AD 0.1

D1609732

HEAVEN IN HONG KONG

Velda Armstrong, orphaned and in charge of her small brother, who is only six years old, is terrified that living in Hong Kong he will be taken from her and put into an Orphanage.

Although they are desperately poor, she wishes him to go to school and is told though her father was known and respected as the Headmaster, she has to have a Sponsor.

She cannot think who to ask and then is told that her father once saved the life of the most important Trader in the East – Mike Medway.

He is an amazing personality and owns more private ships than anyone else in the East.

She goes to see him on his magnificent Junk – *The Sea Dragon* and he agrees to sponsor Jimmy.

At the same time, because she is so lovely, he suggests he should also look after her.

Frightened and shocked by such a suggestion she runs away and he realises for the first time in his life he has to woo a woman, rather than having her fall eagerly into his arms.

How he cleverly persuades Velda that he is indifferent to her.

How he then decides to forget her and goes to Japan to enjoy himself with the Geisha Girls and how he returns to Hong Kong to find Velda is dying is all told in this exciting and unusual story which is the 431st by Barbara Cartland.

HEAVEN IN HONG KONG

BARBARA CARTLAND

SEVERN HOUSE PUBLISHERS

This first world edition published in Great Britain 1990 by
SEVERN HOUSE PUBLISHERS LTD of
35 Manor Road, Wallington, Surrey SM6 0BW
Simultaneously published in the U.S.A. 1990 by
SEVERN HOUSE PUBLISHERS INC, New York

British Library Cataloguing in Publication Data
Cartland, Barbara *1902–*
  Heaven in Hong Kong.
  I. Title
  823.912

  ISBN 0–7278–1711–X

Distributed in the U.S.A. by
Mercedes Distribution Center, Inc.
62 Imlay Street, Brooklyn, New York 11231

Printed and bound in Great Britain by
Bookcraft [Bath] Ltd.

AUTHOR'S NOTE

When the small island off the China Coast called Hong Kong was acquired by the British, Queen Victoria was delighted.

She wrote to King Leopold of the Belgians in 1841 saying:

'Albert is so much amused at my having got the island of Hong Kong.'

The Foreign Secretary, Lord Palmerston, considered it a white elephant and a massive mistake on the part of Britain's Superintendant of Trade in China who had negotiated the deal.

In a letter to the unfortunate Captain Charles Elliot he wrote:

'A barren island with hardly a house on it.'

Nevertheless, the British began trading with China on a regular basis and ships arrived annually from the East Indian Company which was based on the Indian Coast.

Trade began to flourish which was mainly in China's favour because the silk and tea that she sent to Hong Kong had to be paid for in silver.

In 1851 the colonist population had risen to a mere 33,000.

However, it had begun to be of great importance as a trading centre.

The invasion of China by Japan in 1931 brought the population up to 800,080 and after the war between

China and Japan in 1937 another 700,000 people fled to Hong Kong.

At the time I have written this novel, Hong Kong was becoming of great interest to the British and small though it was an important part of the Empire.

Wherever they went, the British took with them their equestrain sports, their race courses and cricket grounds, their class difference and their religion.

The spire on the Church of St. John in the words of James Morris in Pax Britanica was:

'Like the minaret of a mosque, it represented more (or less) than a faith: it was the emblem of a society, expressing temporal as well as spiritual values, and clearly built upon the assumption that if God was a church-goer at all, he was obviously C. of E.'

ABOUT THE AUTHOR

Barbara Cartland, the world's most famous romantic novelist, who is also an historian, playwright, lecturer, political speaker and television personality, has now written over 460 books and sold nearly 500 million copies all over the world.

She has also had many historical works published and has written four autobiographies as well as the biographies of her mother and that of her brother, Ronald Cartland, who was the first Member of Parliament to be killed in the last war. This book has a preface by Sir Winston Churchill and has just been republished with an introduction by the late Sir Arthur Bryant.

'Love at the Helm' a novel written with the help and inspiration of the late Earl Mountbatten of Burma, Great Uncle of His Royal Highness The Prince of Wales, is being sold for the Mountbatten Memorial Trust.

She has broken the world record for the last twelve years by writing an average of twenty-three books a year. In the Guinness Book of Records she is listed as the world's top-selling author.

Miss Cartland in 1978 sang an Album of Love Songs with the Royal Philharmonic Orchestra.

In private life Barbara Cartland, who is a Dame of Grace of the Order of St. John of Jerusalem, Chairman of the St. John Council in Hertfordshire and Deputy President of the St. John Ambulance Brigade, has fought for better conditions and salaries for Midwives and Nurses.

She championed the cause for the Elderly in 1956 invoking a Government Enquiry into the 'Housing Conditions of Old People'.

In 1962 she had the Law of England changed so that Local Authorities had to provide camps for their own Gypsies. This has meant that since then thousands and thousands of Gypsy children have been able to go to School which they had never been able to do in the past, as their caravans were moved every twenty-four hours by the Police.

There are now fourteen camps in Hertfordshire and Barbara Cartland has her own Romany Gypsy Camp called Barbaraville by the Gypsies.

Her designs 'Decorating with Love' are being sold all over the U.S.A. and the National Home Fashions League made her, in 1981, 'Woman of Achievement'.

Barbara Cartland's book 'Getting Older, Growing Younger' has been published in Great Britain and the U.S.A. and her fifth Cookery Book, 'The Romance of Food', is now being used by the House of Commons.

In 1984 she received at Kennedy Airport, America's Bishop Wright Air Industry Award for her contribution to the development of aviation. In 1931 she and two R.A.F. Officers thought of, and carried, the first aeroplane-towed glider air-mail.

During the War she was Chief Lady Welfare Officer in Bedfordshire looking after 20,000 Service men and women. She thought of having a pool of Wedding Dresses at the War Office so a Service Bride could hire a gown for the day.

She bought 1,000 gowns without coupons for the A.T.S., the W.A.A.F.s and the W.R.E.N.S. In 1945

Barbara Cartland received the Certificate of Merit from Eastern Command.

In 1964 Barbara Cartland founded the National Association for Health of which she is the President, as a front for all the Health Stores and for any product made as alternative medicine.

This has now a £500,000,000 turnover a year, with one third going in export.

In January 1988 she received 'La Medaille de Vermeil de la Ville de Paris', (the Gold Medal of Paris). This is the highest award to be given by the City of Paris for ACHIEVEMENT – 25 million books sold in France.

In March 1988 Barbara Cartland was asked by the Indian Government to open their Health Resort outside Delhi. This is almost the largest Health Resort in the world.

Barbara Cartland was received with great enthusiasm by her fans, who also fêted her at a Reception in the city and she received the gift of an embossed plate from the Government.

OTHER BOOKS BY BARBARA CARTLAND

Romantic Novels, over 400, the most recently published being:

A Kiss From A Stranger
A Very Special Love
A Necklace of Love
A Revolution of Love
The Marquis Wins
Love is the Key
Free as the Wind
Desire in the Desert
A Heart in the Highlands
The Music of Love
The Dream and the Glory (In aid of the St. John Ambulance Brigade)

The Wrong Duchess
The Taming of a Tigress
Love Comes To The Castle
The Magic of Paris
Stand and Deliver Your Heart
The Scent of Roses
Love at First Sight
The Secret Princess
Heaven in Hong Kong
Paradise in Penang

Autobiographical and Biographical:

The Isthmus Years 1919–1939
The Years of Opportunity 1939–1945
I Search for Rainbows 1945–1976
We Danced All Night 1919–1929
Ronald Cartland (With a foreword by Sir Winston Churchill)
Polly – My Wonderful Mother
I Seek the Miraculous

Historical:

Bewitching Women
The Outrageous Queen (The Story of Queen Christina of Sweden)
The Scandalous Life of King Carol

The Private Life of Charles II
The Private Life of Elizabeth, Empress of Austria
Josephine, Empress of France
Diane de Poitiers
Metternich – The Passionate Diplomat

Sociology:

You in the Home	Etiquette
The Fascinating Forties	The Many Facets of Love
Marriage for Moderns	Sex and the Teenager
Be Vivid, Be Vital	The Book of Charm
Love, Life and Sex	Living Together
Vitamins for Vitality	The Youth Secret
Husbands and Wives	The Magic of Honey
Men are Wonderful	The Book of Beauty and Health

Keep Young and Beautiful by Barbara Cartland and
Elinor Glyn
Etiquette for Love and Romance
Barbara Cartland's Book of Health

General

Barbara Cartland's Book of Useless Information with a
Foreword by the Earl Mountbatten of Burma. (In aid of
the United World College)
Love and Lovers (Picture Book)
The Light of Love (Prayer Book)
Barbara Cartland's Scrapbook (In aid of the Royal
    Photographic Museum)
Romantic Royal Marriages
Barbara Cartland's Book of Celebrities
Getting Older, Growing Younger

Verse:

Lines on Life and Love

Music:

An Album of Love Songs sung with the Royal
Philharmonic Orchestra.

Films

The Flame is Love
A Hazard of Hearts

Cartoons:

Barbara Cartland's Romances (Book of Cartoons) has
recently been published in the U.S.A., Great Britain, and
other parts of the world.

Children:

A Children's Pop-Up Book: 'Princess to the Rescue'

Cookery

Barbara Cartland's Health Food Cookery Book
Food for Love
Magic of Honey Cookbook
Recipes for Lovers
The Romance of Food

Editor of:

'The Common Problem' by Ronald Cartland (with a
preface by the Rt. Hon. the Earl of Selborne, P.C.)
Barbara Cartland's Library of Love

CHAPTER ONE

1880

Velda came into the house pulling her hat off as she did so.

The room, as she expected, was empty.

She looked out of the window to see her small brother Jimmy playing with two Chinese children in the yard.

She looked at them for some minutes.

Then with a deep sigh she sat down at the table which she called her deck.

She drew some papers out of the pocket of her short coat.

She studied them, although she knew already what they contained.

'Who shall I ask?' she murmured beneath her breath.

Because there seemed to be no answer, she rose and went to the front door through which she had just entered.

Below her the land sloped away down to the water of Hong Kong harbour.

Without really realising it, the beauty of the sun glittering on the sea, the junks, dhows, fishing boats and trading ships from all over the world gave her a feeling of happiness.

It was something beauty always did wherever she found it.

But nothing, she thought, could be more beautiful than Hong Kong whose name meant 'Fragrant Harbour'.

Then, as if she needed inspiration from another source, she looked to where in the distance she could see the Church of St. John.

It stood in a wide Churchyard above the waterfront and was, as she knew, in the very best part of the town.

There was Government House on one side of it and Flagstaff House on the other.

Not far away were the Barracks, the Parade-ground and the cricket field.

Behind were the steep streets leading up to the most fashionable residential area.

Towering above it was the Peak which was tawny and brown, while there was a riot of colour from the gardens of the richest residents.

'I love Hong Kong,' her mother had said when they first came there.

Over the years she had never changed her mind.

But their life had changed and so had the place where they lived.

It was Velda's father, the dashing Ralph Armstrong who had left the Navy to come to Hong Kong to make his fortune.

'There is far more money in trading,' he had said to his wife and daughter, 'than I shall ever earn in the service of my country.'

Because Ralph Armstrong always had his own way, they had left the comfortable house where they lived in England.

Velda could still feel the thrill of going East.

It was her father, always the optimist, who had believed firmly that, whatever the difficulties, something would turn up.

He rented a large house outside the capital town, Victoria.

Near what was known as Aberdeen, it seemed almost like the English countryside.

There were trees, shrubs, birds and flowers.

Everything, however, was a thousand times more beautiful than Velda could ever have imagined it would be.

At first things had gone exactly as Ralph Armstrong had predicted they would.

Because he was very knowledgeable about ships he was given command of a fast and very up-to-date cargo vessel.

He carried spices, rice and a dozen different commodities to other ports and, as he had told his wife and daughter, he was making money.

He could not spend a great deal of time with his family, but he always brought his ship back to Hong Kong.

Then, three years later, on a voyage home, he was set upon by the pirates who lurked amongst the islands.

In defending his crew, his goods and his ship, Ralph Armstrong lost his life.

To his wife it was a blow from which she never recovered.

Lacking the will to live, she had caught a fever and died two years after her husband.

She had loved Ralph Armstrong overwhelmingly from the moment when they first ran away together.

They had been forbidden by his family to marry.

Her whole life had centred round him.

On his death she found that he had neglected to insure his life and his debts were far greater than she had expected.

She and her two children were forced to leave the comfortable house outside Victoria.

They moved into a small, cheap building which was little

more than a hut in what was the Chinese Quarter.

Jimmy, who had been born, as his father often said, as an 'afterthought', was by this time nearly seven years old.

He was too young to worry about where he was, or where he went, so long as he was with his mother and sister.

It was Velda who minded the discomfort of their new home and missed the garden with its shrubs and flowers.

The furniture, pictures and nearly everything else was sold in order to pay off her father's debts.

But Mrs Armstrong had an unquenchable courage.

Although she wept every night for the husband she had lost, she knew she must protect and provide for her children.

'We have to make money somehow, darling,' she said to Velda.

'How can we do that, Mama?' Velda asked.

Her mother had thought for a long time before she decided she could teach.

It was the Chinese who made her think of having a small School of her own.

She could teach those who wished to serve the richer residents of Hong Kong how to speak English.

They paid what they could afford, which was very little.

Velda knew that in many cases they went on owing money indefinitely.

But her mother could not harden her heart and turn them away.

'They are so eager to learn, dearest,' she said, 'and they realise that to speak even a little English will give them a better job than if they do not understand a word of what they are told to do.'

'But we also need money, Mama,' Velda replied.

Her mother smiled.

4

'They will pay me when they can.'

It was the same optimism her father had when he would say that 'something would turn up'.

Velda knew it was no use arguing.

She just had to accept what her mother thought was simple Christian kindness.

At the same time, when they went short of food she found herself worrying about the future.

Most of all she worried about Jimmy.

She felt he should be with boys of his own nationality.

She knew too that he must be properly educated if he was to have a chance of attending a Public School.

Ralph Armstrong had been at Eton as well as Oxford, where he had met his wife.

He had joined the Navy because he wanted to see the world.

He was an extremely intelligent man and had risen quickly to the rank of Senior Lieutenant.

But when he was given command of a merchant ship in Hong Kong he called himself 'Captain'.

So did everybody else who knew him.

Whatever his rank, there was no pension for somebody who had left the Navy of his own accord.

Not any pension from those for whom he had been working when he was killed.

Velda and Jimmy were orphans.

Looking again at the ships moving below her in the harbour, Velda asked the same question:

'Who shall I ask?'

Then from a ramshackle hut at the side of the yard there appeared a man, who came hobbling towards her.

Bill Down had been a sailor but had lost a leg in an engagement at sea.

Attached to the stump was a wooden crutch which

enabled him to walk with the help of a stick.

'Oi sees ye've come back, Miss Velda,' he said. 'Will they tak' Master Jimmy?'

He reached Velda's side as he finished speaking.

'That is something I want to talk to you about, Bill,' Velda answered.

He smiled and sat down on a wooden bench which stood outside the door.

'Oi've bin thinkin'' he said, as she did not continue, 'they'll ask too much money for ye to be able to find it.'

'I will find it somehow!'

She spoke with a determination that made her voice ring out.

Bill shook his head.

'Ye loike y'father,' he said. 'Once he'd made up 'is mind, there'd be nothin' no one could do 'bout it.'

Bill had been with the Armstrongs ever since they had come to Hong Kong.

He had attached himself to them when they were living in the country.

Without having been engaged as such he had constituted himself gardener, odd-job man and guardian.

He was always there.

It had been a comfort to be able to leave the house knowing he would look after everything.

They soon began to rely on him.

He had immense admiration for 'the Captain', with whom he had served on several voyages.

He loved the children.

Mrs Armstrong often said he was better than any Nanny in the way he looked after Jimmy.

When they had to move into Victoria, Bill went too.

There was no room for him in the little house and he could not afford the rent of the houses near them.

6

With the help of a few Chinese boys he built himself a hut in the yard.

When the Winter came he covered the leaky roof with a piece of tarpaulin.

It had come from a boat in the harbour.

'How can he possibly live in such discomfort?' Velda had asked her mother.

Both knew however that Bill was indispensable.

They would find it hard to manage without him.

Now that Mrs. Armstrong was dead, Bill was the only person Velda could talk to about their troubles.

Now she sat down on the doorstep and said:

'They will take Jimmy because the Head Master knew Papa, and he will be prepared to reduce the fees a little.'

'That be good noos, Miss Velda!' Bill said with relish.

'That is what I thought,' Velda agreed, 'but there is a condition.'

'An' wot moight that bee?'

'They insist that I must have somebody to guarantee or sponsor Jimmy! I know of no one I could ask to do that.'

Bill looked at her with a worried expression on his face.

He knew, because they had discussed it before, that Velda was always afraid that somebody in authority would consider Jimmy was not being properly cared for.

This meant he would have to go into an Orphanage.

An unchaperoned girl of eighteen would not be deemed a suitable Guardian to have charge of an English boy in a foreign land.

Hong Kong had become part of the British Empire in 1842.

There was inevitably a large number of good people determined to introduce the English way of life.

They considered it essential in what they thought of as an 'outlandish' part of the world

The English invariably created on 'heathen' soil the customs and the morality that they believed was the emblem of English Society.

In Cheltenham, Harrogate and Bournemouth, Christian women sewed diligently ugly Mother Hubbards to cover the nakedness of women and children in Africa.

In Hong Kong the proprieties grew with the prosperity of the Colony.

The old East India Company had established several Orphanages in different parts of the East.

One had been opened in Hong Kong.

It had been built for the children of employees who had lost their parents through one reason or another.

Every time she looked at the gaunt grey building not far from St. John's Church, Velda shivered.

She knew that if they took Jimmy from her she would lose the last link with her family.

Besides which she could not bear for him to be without the happiness of his home, however hungry he might be.

'Who can I ask to sponsor Jimmy?' she said to Bill and there was a desperate note in her voice.

Bill scratched his head.

His sparse hair was growing white.

Because he had often suffered a great deal of pain he looked older than his fifty years.

'There be t'Clergy,' he said after a moment.

Velda shook her head in horror.

'No, no! Not the Clergy! You know as well as I do that they would think it was for Jimmy's good that he should be placed in an Orphanage.'

She sighed and went on:

'Or perhaps he might be adopted by one of those old ladies who think they are being kind to the Chinese children when they force them to attend Sunday School!'

Bill was silent.

He knew there were a number of Englishwomen who were always trying to convert the Chinese.

They were perfectly happy with their own religion and its profusion of Gods and Goddesses.

'Then who be there . . . ?' Bill started to say.

Then he gave a sudden shout:

'Oi've got it! Oi knows who ye must ask!'

'Who?' Velda enquired.

'Mr Medway – that's who!'

'Do you mean Mike Medway?' Velda asked in a tone of astonishment.

'That Oi does! Oi knows it'd be a good thing fer Master Jimmy to be – wot ye call it – sponsored by 'im!'

'But . . . how can I ask Mr Medway . . . I do not even know him!' Velda exclaimed.

As she spoke she thought she might not have met Mike Medway, but there was no one in Hong Kong who did not know of him.

He was the most notorious, the most talked-about and the most outstanding personality in the whole place.

She had often heard her father and mother's friends discussing him.

When she and her mother had moved into the town they did not entertain in what was the Chinese area.

They could not afford it.

Even so, Velda continued to hear about Mike Medway from Bill.

His parties were notorious, and the English residents waited breathlessly for invitations.

The Chinese watched from the wharf with delight.

Apart from his more formal but still unusual and amazing parties, Mike Medway entertained in a different way.

9

It was whispered about in Drawing-Rooms and laughed about in the Hong Kong Club to which every gentleman belonged.

Bill told Velda about wild evenings when Mike Medway invited his men-friends to meet the most alluring women.

Women who would certainly not have been accepted by their wives.

Velda could remember about *Pretty Pearl*.

She was a Chinese girl of such beauty that men were bowled over by her immediately she appeared.

'Mr Medway's 'ung 'er wiv pearls from 'er neck to 'er feet!' Bill revealed with relish.

'That must have been very expensive!' Velda remarked.

Bill snapped his fingers.

'What's expensive to Mr Medway? 'E's that clever – everythin' 'e touches turns t'gold.'

Velda listened attentively, and Bill went on:

'An' the women knows it! There's another beautiful girl 'e brings back from Sinagpore. 'Alf Australian she be, an' 'alf Malay. Ain't no words to describe 'ow gorgeous she be!'

'And does he also give pearls to her?' Velda enquired.

Bill laughed.

'Oi 'ears as Di'monds is wot she craves for. That's why they've christened 'er *Di'mond Lil'*!'

He laughed again before he went on:

After these parties Velda heard there were always fireworks, with the Chinese watching from the wharf.

Two months ago, the last one had taken place.

Velda had allowed Jimmy to stay up so that he could watch the colourful display as the rockets exploded in the sky.

Those which sprayed down on the junks looked like fountains.

10

He had stood on the bench where Bill was sitting now, clapping his hands with delight.

He had almost cried when the fireworks were over.

Velda said it was time he went to bed.

'There will be more fireworks next time Mr Medway gives a party,' she had promised, 'and I will wake you up so that you can see them.'

'I hope he will come back soon,' Jimmy had murmured.

He was so tired that he had fallen asleep almost as soon as Velda tucked him in.

Now it seemed to her extraordinary that Bill should suggest that Mr Medway, of all people, should sponsor Jimmy at the School.

Of course it was impossible.

Still, she was curious as to why the old sailor should have though of the idea.

''E'll do it – Oi knows 'e'll do it!' Bill was saying. 'One thing's sure about Mike Medway, an' no one can deny it – 'e always pays 'is debts!'

'Pays his debts?' Velda echoed. 'What do you mean by that?'

Bill looked at her in surprise.

'Yer father must 'ave told ye that 'e saved Mr Medway's life when 'e were a boy?'

'No, I have never heard of it,' Velda replied. 'Is it true?'

'Corse it be true!' Bill said. 'Oi were on t'ship when it 'appened, an' we was roight proud o' our Skipper – that we were!'

'Please, tell me about it,' Velda begged.

It seemed extraordinary to Velda that she had never heard the story before.

Yet it was like her father not to boast of anything he had done but to leave it to others to do it for him.

11

'Well – t'were loike this,' Bill began.

He paused for a moment as if thinking back.

'We was in Singapore 'arbour in one o' th' Naval ships yer father was in charge of – an' very proud 'e were of it – insistin' everythin' be "ship-shape 'n Bristol fashion".'

Velda settled herself a little more comfortably on the doorstep.

She knew how long-winded Bill could be when he was telling a story.

He would go off in all directions before he got to the point.

'We was just 'bout ready t'set sail when an order comes from 'Ead Quarters that we was t'take aboard some equipment as was wanted in another port. Oi can't tell ye now 'xactly wot it were.'

He scratched his head, then, as if it was unimportant, went on:

'Whatever it were we was to carry it. Large and proper tricky t'er move, us started to swing it on deck.'

Velda longed to ask questions, but she knew it was better to let Bill continue without interruption.

He went on:

'There be a young boy aboard as 'ad come with 'is father, who was a friend o' your Dad's. The two men was a-talkin', and the young lad – 'bout eleven or twelve 'e was, was watchin' us bring a huge case off th' quay.'

He paused to draw in his breath before he continued:

'Well, Oi don't rightly know what 'appened, but somethin' broke, an' as it did so yer father, quick as a flash, seizes the boy throws 'im down on the deck, an' lies on top of 'im.'

Velda gave a little exclamation.

''E be only jest in time,' Bill went on, 'Th's packing-case landed on th'spot where th'lad 'ad been standin'!'

'But nobody was hurt?' Velda asked breathlessly.

'Nobody, an' loike a miracle it were, that they gets away with it!'

'So that is how Papa saved Mr Medway's life!'

''E'd 'ave bin squashed flat as a pancake if th'case 'ad fallen on 'im!' Bill said.

'As t'were, yer father picks 'imself up, laughs an' takes the boy an' 'is father below for a drink, an' if ye asks me – they needs it!'

Velda was looking down at the harbour with unseeing eyes.

The story Bill had just told her changed everything.

She knew without being told that if Mike Medway, of all people sponsored the introduction of Jimmy to the School, they would be only too pleased to take him.

To men like the Head Master, and a great many other people in Hong Kong, it was Mike Medway's money that talked.

They did not concern themselves with any other aspect of his life.

'Wot Oi be suggestin',' Bill was saying, 'is that soon as 'e comes into 'arbour – an' Oi'll find out when – ye goes t'see 'im. When 'e 'ears as Master Jimmy be your father's son, Mike Medway'll pay 'is debt, or Oi'll eat me 'at!'

'It is certainly an idea,' Velda said quietly, 'so do find out, Bill, when he will next be here.'

She went into the house as she spoke.

She felt that Bill had put an idea into her mind that was rather hard to assimilate.

Never had she thought in her wildest dreams that she would meet Mike Medway.

Since her parents had died she had grown used to speaking to no one except for Bill and the Chinese she taught in her mother's place.

13

It had taken up almost all her time.

She had never worried about taking part in any of the activities in which the other Colonial houses were interested.

She heard about them from Bill who always knew the latest gossip.

But while she was not worried about herself, she was concerned for Jimmy.

He was now six years and eight months old.

She knew it was wrong that he had no playmates who were English.

She had taught him the simple subjects.

But there were those about which she herself knew very little.

Her mother had been an extremely well-educated woman.

In England Velda had Governesses and Tutors.

It had been difficult to find competent persons in Hong Kong.

It was impossible therefore for Velda not to realise that Jimmy must have a proper education.

The School, which had been open for less than a year, was, she thought, exactly the right place for him.

She had heard, again through Bill, that they were very particular about whom they accepted.

Only the sons of the English residents in Hong Kong were taken as pupils.

It crossed Velda's mind that, if Jimmy received the hospitality of his School-friends, it would not be possible for her to return it.

This, however, was a bridge she had no wish to cross at the moment.

All she was concerned with was Jimmy's education.

She hoped that he would be clever enough, when the

14

time came, to gain a place at Eton.

She had no idea where the money for that was to come from.

It would be even more difficult, to take him back to England.

Like her father, she thought that 'something would turn up', and when it did, she must be prepared.

Looking out into the yard at the back she could see Jimmy chasing a small Chinese boy round and round.

Both of them were shouting with laughter.

He looked happy, although like herself, he was rather thin.

They were obliged to eat sparsely.

But she thought nobody could think that Jimmy was not the son of an English gentleman.

His fair hair, his blue eyes, his clear complexion and his irresistible charm had all been inherited from his father.

'He *must* go to School – he *must!*' she told herself.

It all depended on Mike Medway.

That evening Bill came back with the information that Mike Medway was due in harbour in two days' time.

'Are you sure?' Velda asked.

She found it hard to believe that because she needed him so badly he was going to appear so quickly.

'That's wot they tells me,' Bill said, 'an' th' Chinese, as ye knows, is "opin" there'll be fireworks!'

'Jimmy will enjoy that!' Velda smiled.

'As will th' young women 'e arranges 'em for!' Bill said laconically.

'Does he only have fireworks when they are present?' Velda asked.

'It be women as loikes plenty o' noise an' excitement,' Bill said. 'Men enjoys drinkin' Mr. Medway's wine, an' tryin' to take 'is money off 'im at th' gambling-tables.'

'Gambling!' Velda exclaimed.

''E 'as card-games, an' that there game where a little ball runs round a wheel. They sez 'undreds o' dollars changes 'ands night after night!'

It all sounded very strange to Velda.

What was more, it frightened her that she should have to beg a favour from such a man.

'Has Mr. Medway never been married?' she asked unexpectedly.

Bill looked at her in surprise.

'Ain't ye 'eard that 'bout 'im?' he asked.

'Heard what?' Velda enquired.

'That 'e were married when 'e were quite a young man t' an English Lady, daughter of a Earl 'er was.'

Velda looked surprised.

'That happened to her? Did she leave him?'

'Nah, it weren't nothin' loik that,' Bill said. ''Er went mad!'

'Mad?' Velda exclaimed.

'That's roight. Orf 'er 'ead, so to speak, an' 'er 'ad to be shut up in a special 'Ospital. They sez 'er don't know Mr. Medway 'imself when 'e goes to see 'er.'

'How sad!' Velda exclaimed. 'Where is she?'

'In England, an' Oi 'ears 'e never speaks of 'er an' people knows better than t' mention it!'

'Of course,' Velda agreed. 'It must be terrible for him. So he has no children?'

'Oi can't imagine Mike Medway with children! Oi can't see 'em mixin' with *Pretty Pearl* or *Di'mond Lil* – can ye?'

'I . . . I suppose . . . not,' Velda replied.

16

When she went to bed she was thinking that it was sad for any man, however rich, to have a wife who was mad.

Also he had no son to inherit his great wealth.

She was feeling sorry for Mike Medway.

Then she laughed.

Why should she feel sorry for a man who was admired, applauded and undoubtedly ruled the world in which he moved?

She had a sudden longing to find somebody else to sponsor Jimmy.

Anyone, she thought, rather than she should have to remind Mike Medway of his debt to her father.

She had no wish to plead with him for it was something completely outside her ordinary way of life.

Then she told herself she was being absurdly over-sensitive about it.

After all, all he had to do was to write a short note to the Head Master of the School.

Then he could forget about it and go back to his amusements, like *Pretty Pearl* and *Diamond Lil*.

'I suppose,' she told herself, 'his parties are far more interesting than those given by the Governor, where everybody has to be formal and very careful of what they say.'

Velda was completely ignorant of what sort of parties he gave.

But she could understand that a man who was constantly at sea would need, when he was ashore, to have beautiful women to admire him.

Of course he would play Games of Chance with his men-friends.

He would also enjoy the excitement caused by his fusillade of fireworks.

17

It was as if he was expressing himself.

Perhaps that was what he wanted to do, she thought, express himself, enjoy himself, and have no shadows over his life, like a mad wife.

The fact that everything concerning him was not perfect made him seem more human, instead of being a kind of mystical figure.

'If he does condescend to see me,' she thought humbly, 'at least I shall have met him, and when people talk about him he will mean more to me than a Geni out of a Fairy Story.'

She laughed at her imaginings.

She tried to be very practical about everything, as her mother would have wanted her to be.

Yet she could not help feeling lately that many things in Hong Kong were unreal.

It was impossible to live with a view of the harbour and the ceaseless parade of vessels large and small without feeling she was watching a performance on a stage.

There was, too, the picturesqueness of the Chinese.

Chinese children were lovely.

It was she thought as if they had come down from another Planet to join mere mortals.

When she left the house and walked down to the wharf the *sampans* the men with their pigtails and big beehive hats made it all seem part of a dream.

Now her dream was expanding to include someone she had heard and talked about, but never seen.

She had envisaged him as something like the Archangel who had fallen from Heaven to become Satan.

Or else like one of the strange gods in the Chinese Temples.

'I know when I see him I shall be disappointed,' Velda told herself.

At the same time, at least he would no longer be just a name; a mystery entertainer of beautiful women.

A purveyor of fireworks!

'Mike Medway!'

His name was on her lips as Velda fell asleep.

CHAPTER TWO

Velda left the little house and started to walk down to the wharf.

On the sparkling sea, there were innumerable Chinese Junks their brown sails ribbed like bats' wings.

She was looking forward to seeing the Junk that Mike Medway was using.

Bill had explained to her the way he worked.

When he came into port with a huge cargo-boat filled with the goods he was bringing from China or from other ports, he invariably moved into his special Junk.

It was called *The Sea Dragon*.

As soon as Velda reached the wharf there were boats coming alongside.

The Chinese rickshaw boys were waiting.

Their voices had the strange tinkling lilt of Cantonese and pigeon-English.

As they solicited for clients they cried out:

'Likshaw! Likshaw!'

Coming down to the wharf the streets were so narrow and so full of pedestrians that it seemed impossible that a horse could find its way through them.

There were in the seething crowd soldiers and sailors, Portuguese Priests, Nuns and innumerable Coolies in enormous hats.

As Velda expected, and it always excited her, she saw several rich Chinese riding in palanquins.

They had jade hat buttons and robes of brilliant satin embroidered with gold thread.

What interested her more than anything when she had the time, were the birds of Hong Kong.

Many different species were to be seen for sale in gold-painted cages.

She knew the yellow and green *South China Eye* was a favourite with the small shop-keepers.

Their singing, they had told her mother, made the customers happy.

'Happy people buy more,' they smiled.

Velda walked on.

The air was filled with cries and voices, the clip-clop of wooden shoes and the smell of spicy cooking.

Because she was feeling frightened of what lay ahead she forced herself to concentrate on the shops near the wharf.

There were little bread shops which sold delicious freshly baked *see min bao*.

These were rolls with sweet grated coconut in the centre of them.

She knew how much Jimmy enjoyed them.

She decided that although it was extravagant, she would buy some for him on her way home.

But only, she told herself severely, if Mr. Medway acceded to her request.

Now she came upon the hawkers and pedlars who made a tremendous noise crying out their wares.

Some were selling salted fish, others brooms, joss sticks and blood gelatin.

Others carried large flat rattan cages containing *um chun* which were the timid little brown birds called quails in Europe.

Tiny quail's eggs were, as Velda knew, always included in expensive Chinese soups.

She reached a less-crowded part of the quayside.

Moored alongside it was the largest and most impressive Junk she had ever seen.

It had been painted crimson and its carvings were picked out in gold.

Its bat-like sails were furled and, seeing the bow with its carved Dragon, Velda knew that this was Mr. Medway's special Junk.

It was so large, so impressive, that for one moment she felt panic overtake her.

She wanted to run away and hide in the crowds.

Then she remembered Jimmy and thought all that really mattered was that she should secure his future, at least for the moment.

Drawing a deep breath, she walked up the gangplank.

There was a Chinese seaman on duty at the top of it.

He looked at her enquiringly and she said in a small voice which did not sound like her own:

'Please . . . I wish to . . . Mr. Mike . . . Medway.'

He bowed politely.

At the same time, he looked to where another Chinaman was coming along the deck.

The new man came towards them and asked:

'You wish see Master?'

'Yes, please,' Velda replied.

'You tell me name.'

'My name is Miss Armstrong, and I would be very grateful if I could have a few minutes conversation with Mr. Medway.'

The Chinaman nodded.

'You wait, Missie – I ask.'

He walked away and Velda looked round the deck.

It was so clean, so tidy, so brightly polished that she felt Mr. Medway must expect perfection.

She looked up at the masts and at the exquisite gold carvings over the entrance to what she thought must be the Saloon.

She would have been surprised if she could have heard the conversation taking place inside.

Mike Medway was working at his desk and there was a pile of papers in front of him.

He was in his shirt-sleeves because it was so hot.

He was concentrating on a long document which was written in Chinese.

He prided himself that he could read Mandarin and speak Cantonese as well as his own language.

Yet like all Englishmen, he found the flowery manner in which everything was enveloped extremely irritating.

His servant Cheng, who had been with him for many years, came into the Saloon to stand quietly by his desk.

At last Mike Medway said sharply:

'What is it, Cheng? I am busy!'

'Me know, Master, but Lady here.'

Mike Medway groaned.

'Probably another old lady wanting my money!' he exclaimed. 'I already support every Charity in the whole damned place.'

He gave a deep sigh.

'The only one to which I would willingly subscribe is for the Protection of Men from Importunate Women!'

Cheng laughed.

'Not old lady, Master. Velly plettee girl – Missie Armstlong.'

'A pretty girl certainly sounds better,' Mike Medway remarked. 'Very well, show her in. I will give her five minutes and not a second more.'

Cheng went from the cabin.

With a sigh Mike Medway put down the paper he was reading.

It was always the same.

As he came into port there were invariably queues of vultures wanting something from him.

Then he told himself it was his own fault for being rich.

At least he had enough money to send them away happy.

The door of the Saloon opened and Cheng announced:

'Missie Armstlong, Master!'

Velda came in.

She had a quick impression of a large Saloon furnished with comfortable couches, silk cushions and embroidered stools.

Then when she looked at the man who had risen from his seat she was astonished.

She had expected him to look different and he was different from any other man she had ever met.

But she had not expected him to be so overwhelming and so impressive.

At the same time, he looked raffish, if that was the right word.

He was good-looking, in fact extremely handsome.

But there was something about the squareness of his chin, the firmness of his mouth and the penetrating look in his eyes.

It told her he might in fact be the fallen Archangel who became Satan or the Geni she had imagined him to be.

He was tall and broad-shouldered.

As she moved towards him she thought she could feel his vibrations reaching out towards her.

They were something like the fireworks he let off at his riotous parties.

'Good-morning, Miss Armstrong.'

He held out his hand.

Velda took it and dropped him a little curtsy.

'It is . . . kind of you to see me,' she murmured.

'I have only a few minutes,' Mike Medway said, 'and if you will tell me what you want perhaps I shall be able to help you.'

As he spoke his perceptive eye saw from the condition of her clothes that she was very poor.

What she wore was in good taste, but at the same time the colour of her gown was faded from many washings.

He saw too that the ribbons on her straw hat were frayed and her white gloves had been neatly darned on several fingers.

He knew however that Cheng had not exaggerated when he had said she was very pretty.

Lovely was the right word, he thought, with an unusual beauty he had not seen before.

Her face was pointed and dominated by two very large eyes that were green with flecks of gold in them.

She was too thin, but it accentuated her small straight nose and her perfectly curved lips.

They seemed to be the only colour in her face.

Underneath her broad-brimmed hat he thought her hair was the colour of the sunshine.

He knew it would be impossible for her to be anything other than English.

He indicated a chair in front of his desk, and Velda sat down in it.

She looked at him and he was aware there was a frightened expression in her eyes.

25

He thought it must be because she had come begging for money.

With a smile which women invaribly found irresistible he asked:

'Well? What can I do for you?'

Velda looked down at the gold ink-pot which was just in front of her and said a little hesitatingly:

'I . . . I wondered, Mr. Medway . . . if you remember my father . . . saving your . . . life when you . . . were a young . . . boy?'

For a moment Mike Medway stared at her in surprise.

Then he exclaimed:

'Armstrong! Are you the daughter of Ralph Armstrong?'

'Yes . . . that is . . . right.'

'I have not seen him for some years,' Mike Medway said. 'Have you come to tell me he is ill?'

He thought shrewdly that must be the reason for her visit.

'N.no,' Velda replied. 'My father is dead . . . he died three years ago.'

'I am sorry to hear that,' Mike Medway said. 'He was a charming person, and of course I remember that he saved my life when I went with my father abroad the Destroyer of which he was in command.'

'I hoped . . . you would . . . remember,' Velda said, 'because I . . . wish to ask you to . . . do something for my . . . brother.'

'You have a brother?' Mike Medway asked. 'How old is he?'

He imagined now that the request would be for some employment for the young man.

He wondered if he had any suitable vacancy amongst his many different interests.

'Jimmy is nearly seven years old,' Velda replied, 'and I am very anxious for him to go to the new School which has opened here.'

'*You* want him to go to School?' Mike Medway said. 'Am I to understand that your mother is no longer with you?'

'Mama died six months ago!' Velda answered.

There was a little sob in her voice which she could not prevent.

It told Mike Medway without words how much her mother had meant to her.

'So you and your brother are alone,' he remarked. 'Or have you relatives with you?'

Velda shook her head.

'No . . . we have no relatives in Hong Kong.'

'But you cannot be living entirely alone!' Mike Medway persisted.

Velda gave a little smile.

'You are quite safe. An old seaman who once worked with you in two of your ships looks after us and guards us.'

'What is his name?'

'Bill Dowd. He lost a leg five years ago and can no longer go to sea.'

'I think I remember him,' Mike Medway said. 'At the same time, surely at your age you should have a chaperon?'

Velda laughed and it was a very pretty sound.

'I cannot think of anyone who would wish to chaperon me when I am so busy.'

'Busy?' he enquired. 'What do you do?'

Velda hesitated as if she did not want to tell him the truth.

Then, almost as if without speaking he insisted she should do so, she said:

'After . . . Papa was . . . killed we had very little . . . money and had to . . . leave our house which was outside the town on the way to Aberdeen.'

'So you moved into Victoria. Then what happened?'

'Mama started to teach the Chinese who wanted to learn English.'

'She had a School?' Mike Medway asked.

'Not a very impressive one, but a great number of pupils,' Velda explained. 'And now that she is no longer here . . . I am . . . carrying on her . . . work.'

'Teaching the Chinese to speak English!' Mike Medway said, 'and do they pay you?'

He sounded so incredulous that Velda said in a tone that was almost one of rebuke:

'They pay what they can afford, and as they are very grateful for the lessons they give me enough money for Jimmy and me to . . . live.'

'And where do your lessons take place?' Mike Medway asked.

He knew instinctively from the expression in Velda's eyes that she thought he was being unnecessarily inquisitive.

After a moment she replied:

'We are allowed to go into the Warehouse of one of the Traders . . . it is only occasionally that it is so full of goods that we cannot be . . . accommodated.'

'I see,' Mike Medway said. 'and are you asking me to finance this rather unusual tuition for the masses?'

There was a note of sarcasm in his voice which made Velda sit up.

'Certainly not!' she said sharply. 'What I came to ask you, Mr. Medway, is a very simple request which only concerns my brother Jimmy.'

'In what way?'

28

'I have been to see the Head Master of the new School which only educates English boys and he had agreed because he knew Papa that Jimmy can be a pupil.'

She paused a moment and then continued:

'But he insists he must be sponsored by . . . someone of – authority.'

'And you wish me to be that person,' Mike Medway said.

'If you would be so kind . . . I would be very . . . very grateful and I know . . . if Papa was alive . . . he would be . . . grateful, too.'

'And as you are aware,' Mike Medway said, 'as I am only alive due to your father, it is obviously something I cannot refuse.'

Velda clasped her hands together.

'If you will sponsor Jimmy it will be wonderful, and I promise we will not . . . trouble you . . . again.'

'What about his fees?' Mike Medway asked.

'I will of course see to them.'

'From what you receive from your Chinese pupils?'

She looked away from him and there was a slight flush on her cheeks.

'If Jimmy is accepted at the School, I am sure I can find other things I can do.'

'What sort of things?'

She made a helpless little gesture with her hands, as she said:

'I am not quite certain, but I am sure there are houses where things like linen need repairing, or perhaps people who do not . . . like Chinese . . . cooking.'

'In other words, you intend to make yourself a servant to meet the needs of your brother!'

Now the colour deepened in Velda's cheeks.

She thought for a moment, because he was humiliating her, that she hated him.

Then she told herself that for Jimmy's sake, she must be careful not to antagonise him.

She was, however, aware that he was looking at her in a penetrating manner.

It was almost as if he suspected she was not telling him the truth.

Once again she clasped her hands together and said:

'Please . . . please . . . Mr. Medway . . . sponsor Jimmy and . . . as I have already said . . . I will not . . . trouble you . . . again.'

Before Mike Medway could answer the door opened and Cheng came into the Saloon.

'Midday, Master,' he said, 'have appointment Club fifteen minute.'

'So I have!' Mike Medway replied, 'and I dislike being late.'

He looked at Velda and said:

'I will of course agree to your request, Miss Armstrong, but I have a great many things to discuss with you.'

Velda looked at him in surprise, and he went on:

'I therefore suggest that as I have a number of appointments this afternoon that you dine with me tonight. We can then talk without feeling we are racing against time.'

'Dine with . . . you?' Velda questioned almost beneath her breath.

It flashed through her mind that perhaps Mike Medway would be giving on of his parties of which she had heard so much.

'I . . . I am . . . afraid . . .' she began.

'If you are going to say you have another engagement,' he interrupted, 'I can only tell you that I shall not be in Hong Kong for long.'

30

He stopped speaking and smiled at her.

'Therefore I consider it imperative that you should accept my invitation for this evening.'

She looked at him her eyes very wide and, he thought, frightened.

Then he found he was reading her thoughts.

He knew she was thinking that she had nothing suitable to wear.

'We shall be here alone,' he said as if she had asked the question.

He rose to his feet and added:

'I will fetch you at seven-fifteen.'

'There is . . . no need for . . . you to do . . . that,' Velda said quickly. 'I can find . . . my own way.'

There was a distinct twinkle in Mike Medway's eyes as he said:

'I am afraid, Miss Armstrong, you must allow me to do things my way and as I intend to collect you as my guest from where you are living, you can hardly refuse.'

Because he was standing Velda rose to her feet.

'No . . . no . . . of course not,' she said, 'and thank you very much . . . but I am . . . afraid my house is . . . difficult to find.'

'I am sure my Chinese coachman will know the way,' Mike Medway said confidently, 'so give your address to Cheng.'

He walked towards the door of the Saloon as he spoke.

There was nothing Velda could do but follow him.

As she walked through the door she saw Cheng waiting outside to escort her to the gangway.

'Goodbye, Miss Armstrong, until tonight,' Mike Medway said holding out his hand.

He felt her fingers tremble in his as she curtsied.

31

'Thank you . . . very . . . much,' she said in a breathless little voice.

She found herself walking across the deck explaining to Cheng exactly where the house in which they were living was located.

'You understand the carriage cannot come up to the door,' she said, 'but I will be ready for him to stop on the road above it and will reach the carriage before Mr. Medway will alight.'

Cheng shook his head.

'Master not want that, Missie,' he said. 'You wait inside 'til he knock.'

Velda gave a little sigh.

It seemed, she thought, as if everybody was giving her orders, and she was not allowed to have a will of her own.

But the only thing that mattered was that Mike Medway had said he would sponsor Jimmy.

Her heart was singing as she went down the gangway and onto the crowded busy wharf.

She felt she wanted to dance with the children to the music which the blind musicians were playing.

One was extracting exquisite notes from a violin with a 12″ sound-box, another worked clappers with one hand and strummed a Chinese zither with the other.

'I have done it! I have done it!' she wanted to tell them.

Instead she hurried on to buy three *see min bao* rolls for Jimmy.

When she reached home, Bill was waiting for her.

He knew by her expression and the smile on her lips that she had been successful.

'Mr. Medway agree?'

'He has agreed, Bill and it is all due to you,' Velda said. 'If you had not told me Papa saved his life I would never have dared to approach him.'

' 'E remembered it 'appenin?'

'Yes, indeed, and he said that of course he would sponsor Jimmy. We are lucky . . . so very lucky!'

She moved quickly away from Bill to the yard at the back of the house where she found Jimmy.

He was, as she expected, playing with his Chinese friends.

They were making mud-pies under one of the bamboo trees.

On seeing her, he jumped up and regardless of his dirty hands, flung them round her neck.

'You are back, Velda, you are back! I have missed you!'

'And I have missed you, darling,' Velda said, 'but be careful, your hands are very dirty. If you come into the house, I have something delicious to give you.'

Jimmy walked beside her excitedly.

'What is it?' he asked.

'It is a surprise, and it is something you like.'

When Jimmy saw what she had bought he took a huge bite of the first one.

Then with his mouth full he said:

'Shall I give some to Lo Wu and Yin Sing?'

'That is very kind and thoughtful of you,' Velda said. 'But eat the one you have now. I will keep one for your supper and divide the other among your friends.'

She cut the roll in half and Jimmy ran off to give it to them, still munching his own.

She almost grudged the Chinese children having part of Jimmy's treat.

But she knew because he was so like her father that he always wanted to share anything good with his friends.

She went into her bedroom to look hopelessly at the small amount of clothes there were in the cupboard.

33

The gowns were all very much the same as the one she was wearing.

They were faded with washing and threadbare from having been worn constantly over the last two years.

She had also used her mother's clothes as they were much the same size.

Now she looked to see if there was anything in which Mike Medway would not be ashamed of her.

She could not help thinking of *Pretty Pearl* and her strings of pearls.

Then there was *Diamond Lil* sparkling with diamonds at her neck and round her wrists.

Because the comparison was so ridiculous she laughed.

'He will just have to take me as I am,' she thought, 'and if I put him off his dinner, he need never see me again after tonight.'

Finally, she chose a simple gown which had been her mother's.

It was, however, not intended for the evening.

It was more what a Lady would wear for afternoon tea.

It was certainly less threadbare than everything else she possessed.

When Velda put it on she had no idea that the way it clung to her figure and swirled out below her knees made her look very graceful.

She had never been out to dinner before.

She had therefore never troubled to arrange her hair in a fashionable style.

Now she tried to remember how the smart women she saw in the streets styled theirs.

It was not easy because they wore hats and it was not possible to see what they had done to the top of their heads.

Finally she swept back her golden hair in very much the same way as she always did it.

This was a chignon at the back of her head.

However hard she tried to keep her hair looking neat, because it was naturally curly, little tendrils always escaped to soften the line of her oval forehead.

She had put Jimmy to bed before she had started to dress.

Bill had promised to stay in the house until she returned.

"Course Oi will!' he had said when she asked him. 'Ye just go an' enjoy yerself wi' Mr. Medway.'

'I hope to,' Velda said, 'but he is rather frightening.'

'Then just think ye're havin' a real dinner fer once. It might 'ave to last ye th' next day or two.'

Velda laughed.

It was the sort of practical suggestion Bill would make, and she thought there was a great deal of truth in it.

'All that matters,' she said aloud because it was uppermost in her thoughts, 'is that Mr. Medway should sign a letter to the Head Master of the School.'

'If 'e said he'd do it – e'll do it!' Bill remarked. 'Just you talk natural to 'im, Miss Velda, 'cause if ye asks me, them women like *Pretty Pearl* an' *Di'mond Lil* ain't got no conversation!'

Again Velda laughed, but she was sure Bill's advice was sound.

When it grew near to seven-fifteen, Bill went up to the rough path which led to the road above them.

Before he left Velda said:

'Suggest that you come to fetch me. It will save him coming down the rough path.'

'Oi'll try,' Bill answered, 'but if ye ask me, Miss Velda, Oi thinks Mr. Medway wants to see where ye live.'

Because it was what Velda was afraid of, she gave a little exclamation of horror.

Then she looked round at the small Sitting-Room.

She had already tidied it.

Yet now, as if for the first time, she realised how poverty-stricken it was.

The furniture left over from the other house because it was unsaleable was rickety.

The covers of the arm chairs had been darned so often that Velda thought there were more darns than material.

There was however, on the floor a good rug but the fringe had gone.

Some roughly made shelves held a large number of books.

They, at least, were mostly in good repair.

Velda had picked some flowers from the side of the road on her way home and had arranged them on the table.

'If he despises the place, there is nothing I can do about it,' she told herself.

At the same time, she was afraid.

She dared not put it into words, but she thought if Mr. Medway saw how poor they were he might think Jimmy was not suitable to be at the School.

The parents of all the other pupils were rich or distinguished.

She suspected she was frightening herself unnecessarily, for Mike Medway had promised to help Jimmy.

The hands of the clock had almost reached the stroke at which he should arrive when she peeped into his room.

It was so small that it contained only a bed, a chair and a narrow chest-of-drawers in which to keep his clothes.

He was asleep.

There was a smile on his lips, as if he was still thinking of the sweet-meat he had eaten for his supper.

She stood looking at him in the last light which came through the window in a rosy haze before the sun sank.

Then she thought she heard a noise outside and shut the door.

She stood waiting in the centre of the room until she was aware that what she had heard was definitely footsteps.

Somebody knocked.

It was then she opened the door to find Mike Medway waiting outside as she expected.

For a moment they just stood looking at each other.

Velda had no idea that the dying sun turned her hair to a halo of gold.

Then with a smile he asked:

'May I come in?'

'Yes . . . yes . . . of course,' Velda said.

She was embarrassed because she had been so bemused at his appearance that she had for the moment, forgotten her manners.

He was wearing evening-dress.

It made him seem taller and certainly much more impressive than he had been this morning in his shirt-sleeves.

His starched shirt-front and bow-tie were all symbols of a world she had never entered.

As he stepped into the house it seemed to shrink and become even smaller than it already was.

He looked around, and she thought he was aware of how shabby everything looked.

Then, to her surprise, he said:

'I see, like me, you love flowers, Miss Armstrong.'

'They are so beautiful in Hong Kong,' Velda replied.

They were both thinking of the frangipani trees, and the crimson, purple and gold of the azaleas which grew everywhere.

Then Mike Medway said:

'I feel you will appreciate the orchids with which Cheng has decorated my dinner-table this evening, so let us go and inspect it.'

'It sounds very . . . exciting,' Velda replied.

They walked up the path to where the carriage was waiting.

She thought that it was in fact, thrilling to be gong out to dinner with the most famous man in Hong Kong.

'It is something I shall always remember,' she told herself.

The carriage was exactly what she had expected.

It was very smart, very comfortable, with two Chinese coachman on the box.

The horses were exactly the type of fine animals Mike Medway would own.

She wanted to stop and pat them, but he helped her into the carriage.

As they drove off, Bill raised his hand to his forehead in a seaman's salute.

The horses had to go slowly through the crowds of Chinese that thronged the narrow streets in that part of Victoria.

Velda was aware that Mr. Medway was looking her and not out of the window.

Without thinking she said:

'I never imagined . . . I never thought . . . that I should ever be having . . . dinner with . . . you!'

'Why not?'

'Because you are one of the most . . . important men in Hong Kong, and I am sure there are . . . thousands of people you should ask before you . . . invite me!'

Mike Medway laughed.

'Are you really so modest? I can assure you, Miss Armstrong, it would be impossible for me to dine with a more beautiful young lady.'

She looked at him in surprise feeling he must be either sarcastic, or else teasing her.

Then when she saw the expression in his eyes, she blushed and turned her head away.

Because there seemed to be a somewhat embarrassing silence, she said quickly:

'I must tell . . . you how much Jimmy . . . like everybody else in Hong Kong . . . enjoys your . . . fireworks.'

'You have watched them?'

'Yes, of course, and I am sure everybody is hoping, like Jimmy, that you will soon give another party.'

'What do you know about my parties?' he asked.

Velda smiled.

'I know everybody talks about them because Bill tells me so. And they are very . . . exciting!'

'And you think they would excite you?'

Velda hesitated.

She was remembering *Pretty Pearl* and *Diamond Lil*.

She thought that, although she would like to see women like that, it would be something of which her mother would not have approved.

Rather than giving him a direct answer, she said:

'As I have never . . . been to a party it is . . . difficult to know . . .exactly what . . . one would be . . . like.'

'You have never been to a party!' Mike Medway exclaimed. 'But surely, having lived here for so long you must have friends?'

'We had friends when we lived outside Victoria and could afford to entertain them,' Velda replied, 'but after

Papa died, Mama thought it would be . . . embarrassing for . . . them to see . . . where we were . . . living.'

She spoke hesitatingly, but Mike Medway knew exactly what she was saying.

To change the subject he said:

'I am afraid there will not be fireworks tonight, but I promise you my Chinese Chef is very skilful.'

He smiled before he went on:

'When I dine on the *Sea Dragon* he always tries to astonish me with his culinary skills.'

'I am sure I shall enjoy every mouthful,' Velda said, 'and if I was a camel I should have no need to eat . . . any more until the . . . end of the week!'

Remembering what Bill had said to her she spoke without thinking.

Mike Medway laughed.

'I have never before met a lovely woman who wished to be a camel! But my experience of the animal is that it is very unpredictable.'

Velda laughed and he said:

'If you are a camel, what animal do you think I resemble?'

'That is easy,' Velda replied. 'You are of course, a Dragon, and you can either be fiery and very frightening, or very kind.'

'I consider that a compliment,' he said, 'and as a Dragon, I will do my best to be kind tonight.'

Velda flashed him a smile.

'That is what I . . . hope you will be . . . but remember . . . where Dragons are concerned . . . I am easily . . . frightened.'

Unexpectedly Mike Medway held out his hand.

Velda put her hand into his without thinking.

His fingers closed over hers and he said:

'I hope tonight you enjoy yourself and are not fright-ened. I will be as gentle as it is possible to be.'

Velda thought he was playing a kind of game with her.

At the same time, she was vividly aware that his fingers seemed to vibrate against her skin.

Too late she remembered that when her mother had gone our to dinner she had worn gloves.

But she had none that were suitable for the evening.

She had the strange feeling that there was something very intimate in the fact that her skin was touching Mike Medways's.

Yet there was something strong and comforting about the way he was holding her hand in his.

He did not release her.

In silence they drove on towards the wharf where *The Sea Dragon* was waiting for them.

CHAPTER THREE

When she went into the Saloon, Velda thought it was even prettier than it had been on the previous day.

But then she had been too frightened really to appreciate it.

She saw what she had not expected; that Mike Medway had extremely good taste.

Her mother had taught her a great deal about furniture.

She was therefore, aware that the chests and tables in the Saloon were all ancient Chinese and very valuable.

There were also cabinets filled with what she was sure were treasures.

The curtains over the large portholes which were more like windows, were of Chinese silk in the same crimson in which *The Sea Dragon* was painted.

There were priceless rugs on the deck.

Velda longed to look at several Chinese pictures, knowing they were very old, and had a spiritual meaning.

Mike Medway, however, indicated a sofa on which she sat down.

Cheng brought in two glasses of champagne on a gold salver.

Velda sipped hers very slowly.

She was aware that, with so little to eat, the wine could easily go to her head.

She realised that Mike Medway had made this Junk his home.

She wondered if he had a house anywhere, but felt too shy to question him about it.

A table which was at the other end of the cabin was laid for dinner for two.

There were long red candles on it which gave a soft, romantic light.

When Mike Medway had finished his glass of champagne Cheng announced that dinner was served.

Mike Medway rose to his feet.

Velda rose too, and put down her glass hoping he would not notice how little she had drunk.

The table, as had promised her, was decorated with small white orchids with tiny pink spots on their petals.

They were so beautiful that she could not resist putting out her hand to touch one.

It was as if she was making sure they were real.

'Yes, of course they are!' Mike Medway said.

Velda looked at him wide-eyed.

'You are reading my thoughts!'

'I find it easy to do so because your eyes are so expressive.'

'Then I shall have to keep them closed,' she said, 'in case there is something I do not want you to know.'

'Have you any secrets you wish to hide from me?' he asked.

'No . . . of course not!' she replied. 'It is just that it is rather an . . . uncomfortable feeling that . . . anyone should . . . know what one is . . . thinking.'

The meal started with tiny handleless cups of jasmine-scented China tea.

With it were small cockles dipped in sauce, slices of *Abalone* or haliotis snails, and pieces of ginger, prawns and quails eggs on a nest of caviare.

Velda had expected Mike Medway to prefer European food.

She thought with delight that she was going to have a Chinese meal.

If it was prepared by a really good cook, it would, she knew, be more delicious than any other cuisine.

Next came ducks and chickens cooked with lotus seeds, chestnuts and walnuts.

As she ate Velda tried to think that, if she was employed as a cook, whether she would be able to copy anything so delicious.

Next there were meatballs wrapped in dough as light as thistledown and fledgling birds with tiny mushrooms.

Velda was beginning to think she could not eat any more.

Then a soup, which always came late in a Chinese meal was put in front of her.

'It is *Yu Tsi Tang* – sharksfin,' Mike Medway said, 'and as I expect you know, a great speciality.'

'It is certainly too expensive to be enjoyed by the Chinese who live where I do,' Velda remarked.

He frowned.

'I do not think that is the right sort of neighbourhood for you or for Jimmy.'

She raised her chin a little.

'It is all we can afford, and we are quite comfortable.'

She thought he was about to dispute this, but when he did not speak she went on:

'The Chinese who live there are the mothers of the children I teach, and they are always very kind to me. One good thing is, I have nothing that anybody would want to steal.'

She tried to speak lightly but Mike Medway was still frowning, and she said after a moment:

'Please do not let us talk about me. I want to hear about the . . . exciting thing you . . . do.'

She paused a moment before she went on:

'And after dinner . . . if you will let me . . . I want to look at the treasures in this beautiful . . . Saloon.'

Mike Medway smiled.

'You are certainly unusual, Velda. Most women I dine with want to talk about themselves.'

Velda realised he had used her Christian name.

Again he read her thoughts as he said:

'I knew your father, and do not think that we should go on with the formality of "Miss" and "Mister".'

'I would feel it was very . . . familiar to call you anything but Mr. Medway,' Velda replied, 'even though everybody in Hong Kong speaks of you as . . . "Mike".'

'So you have no wish to be familiar with me,' he replied. 'Why not?'

It was a question she had not expected and Velda looked at him in consternation.

Then she told the truth.

'You are . . . so distinguished . . . so important and . . . by a great number of people . . . revered. I feel . . . like the Chinese . . . I should . . . kneel to you.'

Mike Medway stared at her for a moment as if he could not believe what he was hearing.

Then he said:

'That is quite the wrong attitude for anyone as beautiful as you. Men should kneel at *your* feet, and you should make it clear from the moment of your acquaintance with them that that is what you expect.'

Velda laughed.

'As I know no men except Chinese, it is an attitude that is unnecessary for me to adopt.'

Mike Medway sat back in his chair and looked at her.

'You worry me,' he said.

'But . . . why?'

'Because you are wasting your beauty in a manner which would not occur to any other young woman of your age.'

Velda was listening, and he went on:

'You should be going to Balls every night and finding you have at least six partners for every dance.'

He paused and went on:

'You should be anxious to return to England so that you can be presented to the Queen, or at least to the Prince of Wales and the Princess Alexandra. You should also be looking for a husband.'

Velda laughed.

'You are making it sound like a Fair Story! You must realise that it is impossible for me to be a conventional débutante, even though Mama sometimes talked about it. And in Hong Kong . . .'

She stopped.

'And in Hong Kong?' Mike Medway prompted.

'They would . . . disapprove if they knew about me . . . living alone . . . without a chaperon . . . and would try to . . . take Jimmy . . . away from . . . me.'

Now there was an unmistakable fear in her voice and Mike Medway said perceptively:

'You are afraid they would put him in an Orphanage?'

Velda drew in her breath.

'That is . . . what terrifies me,' she said in a voice that was hardly above a whisper, 'and why there was no one but . . . you I could ask to . . . sponsor him for . . . the School.'

Mike Medway understood her reasoning.

'We have settled Jimmy's future for the moment,' he said, 'and now we have to think about yours.'

46

'There is . . . no need to worry about me,' Velda said. 'I can look after . . . myself.'

'I very much doubt it!' he remarked.

It was impossible to say any more for at that moment a fish dish was brought to the table.

It was a whole carp covered in sweet and sour sauce.

After that came several sweetmeats.

Then thin slices of orange in syrup which Mike Medway showed Velda how to dip in iced water so that they became a kind of toffee.

It was all delicious to Velda, although long before the dinner came to an end she felt it was impossible to swallow another mouthful.

As they rose from the table she said:

'I feel I want to light a dozen joss-sticks to *Kso Kuan* – the Kitchen God.'

Mike Medway smiled.

'I am sure there is a shrine to him in my Galley.'

'Then I know your Chef is a devoted worshipper of him.'

'I will tell him what you said, and I am sure he will appreciate it,' Mike Medway smiled.

They moved across the Saloon to the sofa.

As they did so, Cheng and two other Chinese boys who had waited on them at dinner removed the table.

As they shut the door, Velda said:

'Before I go home, may I please look at what is in your cabinet? I can see there are many pieces of jade.'

'I shall be delighted to oblige you.'

He did not follow her but sat down in one of the comfortable armchairs watching her.

She opened the glass door.

The jade pieces were fixed so that they would not move or be smashed in a rough sea.

Although she had lived for so long in Hong Kong, Velda had never imagined that jade could range in colour from pure white to clear emerald green.

There was also some of a dark, almost black, colour.

She stroked several pieces very gently with her fingers and said:

'Mama once told me that the Chinese believe jade comes from Heaven, and that it heals the body and gives them immortality.'

'Do you really want to live for ever?' Mike Medway asked in an amused tone.

'We are all immortal,' Velda said without turning her head, 'there is no such thing as death!'

What she said surprised him, and he said:

'Are you telling me that you believe in the Buddhist Wheel of Rebirth?'

'But of course,' she answered. 'There can be no such thing as death in life. and when our bodies are worn out we go on with our talents and our debts until eventually, we reach Nirvana.'

There was a pause before Mike Medway said:

'You surprise me.'

'Why?'

'Because I have never met an English-woman who thinks like that.'

'It is the only possible way by which a human being could have justice,' Velda explained.

Then as she touched the exquisite carving of a lotus in white and pale green she said:

'Jade also keeps away evil thoughts, and if I had a beautiful piece like this I would touch it every day to make certain my thoughts are pure and good.'

'Are you really telling me that you prefer pieces of jade to diamonds?' Mike Medway asked.

48

Velda laughed.

'As I am unlikely to ever possess either, that is an easy question. While diamonds might enhance my appearance, Jade would be better for my soul, and therefore more enduring.'

Again there was a surprised expression in Mike Medway's grey eyes.

But Velda was looking at a coral carving of *Wang Mu* riding above the tides.

Each piece in the cabinet seemed more beautiful than the last, and when she reached the end of them she said with a sigh:

'I must go home, and thank you for letting me see anything so precious as your collection.'

'Are you really in such a hurry to leave me?' Mike Medway asked in a deep voice.

'Bill is staying in the house to look after Jimmy until I return home, and I do not like to keep him up too late.'

She sighed again before she went on:

'The Chinese wake early and are usually very noisy about it.'

She was smiling as she spoke, and again Mike Medway looked surprised.

He had not risen from the chair in which he was sitting but continued to watch Velda as she stood beside him looking around the Saloon.

'I feel this is your home,' she said almost as if she was speaking to herself, 'and because it is so beautiful when you are worried or tired it soothes you as if you were with somebody you love.'

She was not really speaking to him, just thinking it out in her mind.

Having been so much alone, she usually put her thoughts into words.

Mike Medway rose to his feet.

'I have a lot to talk to you about, Velda,' he said, 'because I feel that as I am looking after Jimmy your father would also want me to look after you.'

Velda stared up at him in surprise.

'There is . . . no need for . . . that,' she said a little uncertainly.

'I think there is,' he answered. 'I want to give you a house which is a suitable protection for your beauty and clothes which will frame it and make you even lovelier than you are at this moment.'

His voice deepened:

'We will be very happy together.'

Now her eyes were very wide, and she could only stare at him as if hypnotised.

'You are lovely, Velda!' he said, 'lovelier than anyone I have ever seen!'

As he spoke his arms went round her and his lips came down on hers.

For a moment Velda could not believe it was happening.

As he kissed her she felt a strange sensation she had never known before.

It was like lightning seeping through her body.

Mike Medway felt it too and he drew her a little closer.

It was then she realised what was happening.

With a cry and a violence which took him by surprise, she forced herself free of him.

Before he could realise what was happening, she had run across the Saloon, hesitated for a moment at the door and was gone.

By the time he had followed her she had run down the gangway.

All he had was one glimpse of her white gown as she disappeared among the crowds on the wharf.

It was almost impossible to believe that she had really vanished.

He stared at the moving crowd below as if he thought she might return.

Now he realised he had taken a wrong step.

Perhaps for the first time in his life he had over-estimated his attractions.

Slowly he walked back into the Saloon.

Shutting the door he sat down in the chair in which he had watched her at the cabinet.

He had known then, as he had looked at the slim graceful lines of her body, her long fingers stroking the jade, and the gold of her hair, that she was utterly desirable.

It was true that he had never before seen a woman with such a lovely face.

She had a spirituality that made her quite different from other women.

She might have been one of the goddesses in jade or rose quartz that was in his cabinet.

He knew just as he possessed them, he wanted to possess her.

He had been quite certain when he kissed her that she had never been kissed before.

She would respond to him as every other woman had done.

Usually too quickly, and before he had actually made up his mind that he wanted them.

Instead he had driven Velda away.

He was perturbed lest, as she travelled back alone through the wharfs, she should come to some harm.

'How can I have been such a fool as to frighten her?' he asked himself.

He knew the answer was because he had never come in contact with anyone so young or so unsophisticated.

The only word to describe her was 'pure' and he knew no other 'pure' women.

Mike Medway was a very intelligent man.

He was also, as he liked to think, an extremely competent judge of character.

He therefore admitted honestly that he had made a mistake.

His only excuse could be, he told himself, that he had never met anybody quite like Velda.

As he thought over what had happened he realised he had not only frightened but also shocked her.

She had heard, as she had told him, of *Pretty Pearl* and *Diamond Lil* and he had known other women of the same type.

He guessed, although he was not sure, that she had little or no idea what these sort of women meant to him.

Or to the other men with whom they spent their time.

Velda had known that her mother would not have accepted such women, nor would the majority of English residents in Hong Kong.

'She will doubtless think I was putting her in the same category as them,' Mike Medway told himself.

He got to his feet and walked up and down the Saloon.

'How could I have been such a fool as to rush my fences?' he asked the gods and goddesses staring at him from the cabinet.

He continued:

'Why did I not understand that, because I was helping her, I was a father-figure on whom she could rely rather than a man who desired her?'

It was very late before Mike Medway went to bed.

When he did, he found it hard to sleep.

Velda was breathless by the time she had wound her way out of the wharfs and climbed up to the little house.

Only as she reached the path leading down to the road did she pull herself together and tidy her hair.

She had no wish for Bill to guess what had happened.

'Why was I so foolish as not to expect, after all I have heard about Mike Medway, that he would behave the way he did?' she asked herself.

She knew that if she had thought that she would not have gone to dine with him alone.

She was aware it was incorrect.

She had been so frightened that he would have a party at which she would certainly look like the Beggar Maid standing before King Cophetua.

It had never crossed her mind that she might be upset in a very different way.

When Bill had gone to bed and she was alone she could not help admitting that a man's kiss was very different from what she had imagined.

She had thought it would be something soft and gentle.

But she could still feel the streak of lightning that had swept through her body.

It had given her sensations that were different from anything she had ever felt before.

As she lay on her bed in the darkness she tossed from one side to the other.

She was trying to forget what her first kiss had meant to her.

It was hopeless and she finally admitted it was something she would remember for the rest of her life.

She tried to figure out why he had offered her a house, clothes and said they would be very happy together.

What had he meant?

Insidiously an idea came into her mind, and she thought that if that was what he had meant, it was horrifying.

Was Mike Medway, whom she had only met for the first time today, asking her to be his mistress?

She told herself it was impossible; that she had misunderstood, or else not heard him correctly.

No gentleman would suggest such a thing to her father's daughter.

Perhaps she was wrong to even imagine he had.

She could hear his deep voice telling her she was lovely and feel his strong arms holding her close against him.

His lips had held hers captive.

It had happened and now she felt bewildered, frightened and shocked all at the same time.

Yet she had to concede that she was curious.

Curious as to what he had meant, what he had intended.

She was also curious to know if he really found her as lovely as he had said she was.

She was incapable of deciding what she should do in the future.

Suddenly she sat bolt upright in bed.

Suppose, because she had insulted him by running away without even thanking him for dinner, he refused to sponsor Jimmy?

Suppose he sailed away without doing anything more about it?

She felt herself tremble at the thought.

Then, because she could not help herself, she got out of bed and walked across the Sitting-Room to open the front door.

She went out into the darkness of the night to look down at the harbour.

The stars were brilliant overhead, and the lights from the moving ships were reflected in the still water.

It was late and very quiet.

She looked up at the sky and thought perhaps her fears were groundless.

'Please . . . God . . . do not let him be . . . angry with . . . me,' she pleaded. 'Please . . . please, God . . . let him . . . sponsor Jimmy . . . whatever he may . . . feel about me.'

It was a fervent prayer.

When she looked down at the harbour she wondered if one of the ships stealing away to an unknown destination might contain Mike Medway.

She felt her whole being reach out as if in an effort to stop him from leaving.

She wanted to hold him until he had written the letter to the Head Master.

Then she was praying again; praying in a broken jerky little voice that seemed to be lost in the castness of the star-studded sky and the world below it.

'Please . . . please . . . God . . . please . . . please . . .'

Mike Medway was called early, as he always was, by Cheng.

His first thought, as had been his last before he fell asleep, was of Velda.

As always, if he made a mistake, he was determined to rectify it.

When he wanted something, he would never give up until he had attained it.

As soon as he was dressed, and before he had his breakfast, he went to his writing-table and wrote a note.

When he had finished he put it into an envelope and addressed it to Velda.

He told Cheng to have it delivered immediately.

Then he sat down to breakfast feeling quite certain that everything would fall into place.

Velda was woken as she always was with the chatter of Chinese women in the houses on either side of her and the noise of the children.

They seemed to welcome every day with an irrepressible joy.

Jimmy was also out of bed and asking for his breakfast long before Velda had it ready for him.

'This morning, Jimmy,' she said, 'you must concentrate on your Arithmetic.'

As she put a bowl down in front of him he said:

'I hate Arithmetic!'

'Then you will have to ask your Chinese friends to help you,' Velda said. 'You know how cleverly and quickly they can add up in the shops.'

She stopped talking for a moment to smile at him.

'Whatever you do in the future, you will need to count your money to know how much you are spending.'

She thought as she spoke that was something her father had never done.

That was why he had left such large bills after he was killed.

'I'm going to be very, very rich when I grow up!' Jimmy said, 'just like Mr. Medway. Bill says he's got so much money that he could buy up the whole of Hong Kong if he wanted to.'

'If he could do that,' Velda said, 'then I am quite sure he is very good at Arithmetic.'

She thought it was rather a banal remark.

At the same time, Jimmy was not listening.

She knew with a little sigh that she was going to have a tussle with his lessons.

She taught him every morning after breakfast.

Today was a Chinese holiday, so the children would not come to lessons and she was free.

She was wondering what she and Jimmy could do when there was a knock on the door.

When she opened it there was a Chinese seaman standing there.

She knew at once that he came from Mike Medway.

'Letter for Missie Armstlong,' he said holding it out.

'I am Miss Armstrong,' Velda said. 'Thank you.'

'I wait answer.'

It was what Velda had expected and she moved back into the house leaving the door open.

Jimmy who was still finishing his breakfast, looked at the seaman with wide eyes.

'Does he come from Mr. Medway's ship?' he asked.

Velda did not answer.

She was opening the note.

She thought that Mike Medway's writing was very like himself; strong, determined and well-formed.

For a moment the words seemed to swim before her eyes.

Then she read:

'Dear Miss Armstrong.

I think before I write to the Head Master of the School I should meet your brother.

Will you therefore bring him to luncheon today.

I shall look forward to seeing you both at one o'clock.

Yours sincerely,
Mike Medway'

It was short, and to the point, and Velda told herself logically it was something she might have expected.

She knew however, with a sinking of her heart that she could not meet him – not after last night.

Not after he had kissed her, and she had run away.

She took a sheet of plain writing-paper from a drawer and sat down at the end of the table.

'What is in your letter, Velda?' Jimmy asked.

'Mr. Medway wishes to meet you, and has asked you to luncheon,' Velda replied. 'I will tell you about it in a moment.'

'Am I to go on his Junk?' Jimmy enquired.

Velda did not answer.

He jumped down from the table to go to the door and talk to the seaman.

He asked him a lot about the Junk, where Mr. Medway had been, and where they were going next.

Velda could hear the seaman answering him.

In her flowing hand, for her mother had insisted that her writing should be elegant, she wrote:

'Dear Mr. Medway,

Thank you for asking Jimmy to luncheon, and I will bring him to you just before one o'clock.

I regret that as I have another engagement, I am unable to accept your kind invitation.

I will collect Jimmy at a quarter-to-two.

Yours sincerely,
Velda Armstrong.'

Having read what she had written, she wondered if she should thank him for last night.

Then she thought that what had happened last night was best forgotten.

Her letter was therefore as formal as his.

She put it into an envelope, addressed it, then took it out to the seamen.

He was telling Jimmy about the porpoises they had seen on the last voyage and of the big fish he had caught.

'Will you please give this to Mr. Medway?' Velda said, handing him her letter.

'Take it Master velly quick,' the seaman replied.

He saluted her, smiled at Jimmy and hurried away.

Velda took Jimmy into the house.

'Now listen, darling,' she said. 'You are going to luncheon with Mr. Medway, and it is very important you should be on your best behaviour and answer any questions he may put to you intelligently.'

'What will he ask me?' Jimmy asked.

'I have no idea, but you can talk to him about his ships and the Junk in which you are to have your luncheon, which is very beautiful.'

'Will he let me explore it?' Jimmy enquired.

'I do not know,' Velda answered, 'but please, Jimmy, be very good. You know it is important for him to tell the School that you will be an excellent pupil and of course hold your own with the boys of your age.'

Jimmy considered this. Then he asked:

'Will they be better at Arithmetic than me?'

'They will if you do not try to understand what I am teaching you,' Velda replied.

'All right,' Jimmy conceded, 'I will add up my sums and try to remember those horrid multiplication tables.'

He spoke with a grimace that made Velda want to smile.

She knew how important it was for him to learn at least a few of the subjects he would be taught at School.

59

She had the feeling, although she was not sure, that he was not as knowledgeable at his age as would be expected.

They struggled away at Arithmetic for two hours.

Then Velda dressed Jimmy in what were his best clothes.

Like her own they were worn and in his case, out-grown.

However, she thought as they walked hand-in-hand towards the wharfs that Jimmy was a very good-looking little boy.

He had the same hair, eyes and complexion as his father and what was more, he had Ralph Armstrong's charm.

He had a way of being interested in everything, whether it was people, places or animals.

She had never known her father to be bored or wonder what he could do with himself.

The hours of the day were just not long enough for him because everything was so entertaining and, in his eyes, fascinating.

Because he and her mother had been so happy together the house had always seemed to be filled with love.

The very air vibrated with their happiness.

'Wherever Papa is,' Velda thought, as they pushed their way through the crowds, 'I know he is helping us now. It was through him that Mike Medway is alive, through him that Bill came to work for us, and through him that Jimmy will go to School.'

She could not help a little flicker of hope that perhaps in five years time Mike Medway would help Jimmy go to Eton.

Then she told herself she was looking too far ahead.

A great deal of things could happen before that.

What they were she had no idea.

But at least Jimmy could go to School now and have the right lessons.

He would also meet the right sort of boys who would be his friends.

She need no longer worry so much about him as she had been doing.

She was so intent on her thoughts that she hardly noticed the things they were passing.

Jimmy however, was as usual finding everything exciting and irresistible.

He was admiring the medicine shop where there were, as he had discovered before, row upon row of coloured bottles.

In them were dried sea-horses from the Gulf of Tonkin and bear's gulls from the Highlands of Tibet.

It was a Chinese boy who had pointed out to Jimmy the vipers from the jungles of Knangsi.

He had talked for a long time about having a viper for himself.

The mere idea of this made Velda shudder.

He was still talking about snakes, and if they would find one up on the Peak, when they reached the Wharf, where *The Sea Dragon* was moored.

When Jimmy saw that the figurehead on the bowsprit of the huge Junk was a Dragon he gave a whoop of joy.

'Look, Velda, a Dragon!' he was saying, 'a Dragon!'

With difficulty Velda made him come to the gang-plank.

She handed him over to the Chinese seaman on duty.

'Will you take him to Mr. Medway, please?' she requested.

'I look after young gentleman, Missie,' the seaman replied.

Because she was afraid that Mr. Medway might appear and insist on her having luncheon with them, Velda hurried away.

She had very little shopping to do.

But she knew there would be plenty to look at for the next three-quarters-of-an-hour.

As she moved down the wharf she could see several English gun-boats and a battleship.

They were in contrast to the stately Junks and clumsy dhows.

There were, too, as always dozens of sampans.

In many of them whole families lived, having no other home.

She stopped to watch a woman leaning over the side of a sampan to do her washing.

In another a mother was sitting in the prow feeding her baby while a child who could not have been more than three years old was plucking a chicken.

There was a large hen-coup attached to the side of the sampan.

As always, she found it fascinating.

She moved on to another street where the tops of the houses were so close together that it was almost impossible to see the sky.

Here again there were shops.

Velda spent a long time trying to decide what fish to buy for their supper.

There were red snappers caught off Hainan, sea-bream which had a red swelling between the eyes, lizard-fish with mouths lined with teeth, and Maels sole which was too expensive for her to afford.

Finally, she bought enough fish for the two of them. It was the cheapest obtainable.

She then went to look at yet another bird-shop in which a number of blue magpies were in their cages.

She remembered that blue-birds were said to bring luck.

She longed to buy one so as to be certain that both she and Jimmy would be lucky.

That meant Mike Medway would sign the letter to the Head Master today.

Then she need not worry about it any longer.

But it would be an absurd extravagance.

She therefore only looked at the magpies and hoped that just by being near them she would get her wish.

She walked on to where the streets were more attractive.

There were long narrow coloured pendants and banners hanging from every one of the high houses.

It was here that the richer people lived.

The balconies were festooned with creepers and flowers of every colour which delighted her eye.

However time was passing, and she had no wish for Mike Medway to be bored with Jimmy or find him an emcumbrance.

It was therefore on the stroke of a quarter-to-two that she climbed the gang-plank of *The Sea Dragon*.

'I have come to fetch my brother,' she told the seaman.

He was the same one she had met on their arrival.

'Master say he wish see Missie Armstlong. It important.'

For a moment Velda was tempted to refuse.

But she could hardly leave without Jimmy and Jimmy was with Mike Medway.

As the seaman escorted her across the deck she felt that he had won a point.

She might have known from the very beginning that it would be impossible to defy him.

CHAPTER FOUR

Cheng was standing outside the Saloon as Velda approached.

He opened the door for her.

'Missie Armstlong,' he announced.

Velda moved forward shyly.

She was aware as she did so that Jimmy was laughing.

Mike Medway and Jimmy were sitting at the same table where she had dined last night.

She could see on it a pile of sweetmeats which she knew would delight the small boy.

He had a large chocolate in his hand as he looked up at her.

Mike Medway rose to his feet.

'Good afternoon, Miss Armstrong. I see you are punctual, which I appreciate as I have a lot to do.'

He spoke in a cold voice which was very different from the way he had addressed her last night.

'I've had scruptious luncheon,' Jimmy said before Velda could speak. 'Look at the chocolates!'

She smiled at him.

'Now you must come home,' she said, 'and thank Mr. Medway very much for having you.'

Mike Medway walked to his desk and picked up a piece of paper.

Turning to Jimmy he said:

'I suggest, Jimmy, that while I have a word with your

sister, you ask Cheng, who is outside, to show you the Junk.'

Jimmy gave a cry of excitement.

'Ooh, can I do that? It would be very exciting!'

He gulped down what was left of his chocolate and ran to the door.

As he disappeared Mike Medway, without looking at Velda, said:

'I have here the letter which I have written to the Head Master, which I hope meets with your approval.'

Velda's heart leapt because he had actually written it.

At the same time, she was rather disconcerted by the way he was addressing her.

She took the letter from him and read:

'*My dear Head Master, I understand you are prepared to have the son of Captain Ralph Armstrong as a pupil in your School.*

As Captain Armstrong was a friend of mine to whom I owe a great debt of gratitude for saving my life, I shall be very pleased to sponsor James Armstrong and be responsible for his fees together with any additional expenses you deem necessary for his education.

Yours sincerely,
Michael Medway.'

Velda read it, then said quickly:

'Thank you very much . . . but I cannot . . . allow you to . . . pay for Jimmy's . . . fees. I will pay . . . them.'

Mike Medway frowned.

'I have written the letter,' he said coldly, 'and that is how I intend to send it.'

'Please . . . we cannot be an . . . encumbrance on you
. . . and I . . . insist that Jimmy is . . . my responsibility.'

Mike Medway put the letter down on his desk.

'You are of course, at liberty to choose another sponsor,'
he said, 'but I should point out to you that it will humiliate
Jimmy and he will undoubtedly be teased.'

He paused a moment and then continued:

'He might even be bullied by the other boys when they
learn that his sister is scrubbing floors in order to pay for
his education.'

He spoke scathingly and the colour flared in Velda's pale
cheeks.

There was silence until she said in a very small voice:

'I . . . realise I am . . . being foolish . . . and of course
. . . I am very . . . grateful.'

There was a faint twist to Mike Medway's lips as he
realised he had won the battle.

At the same time, he had the feeling that he had struck
someone fragile, small and very vulnerable.

He picked up the letter and put it into an envelope.

Then he said:

'I feel it is important to establish in the minds of the
people of Hong Kong, who chatter like parakeets, that it
is Jimmy in whom I am interested, rather than yourself.'

Without looking at her he was aware that Velda gave a
startled gasp.

He knew it was something which had never occurred to
her.

'I therefore,' he went on, 'intend to give a fireworks
party for Jimmy in a couple of days to which all the pupils
of the School will be invited to come with their parents.'

Velda gave a little gasp.

'A . . . fireworks . . . p.party?' she stammered.

'Jimmy has assured me that it is something he would

enjoy more than anything else, and I am quite certain that applies to most small boys.'

'But . . . how . . . how can you . . . I cannot . . . let you . . . do anything so . . . marvellous?'

Mike Medway smiled for the first time since she had entered the Saloon.

'I think your father would understand the reason,' he said, 'and so will you, if you think about it.'

Velda clasped her hands together.

'I . . . I can only . . . say thank you . . . thank you!' she said, 'from the . . . bottom of my . . . heart!'

As she spoke it just flashed through her mind that she would look very strange amongst all the smart and distinguished mothers of the other boys.

Mike Medway was watching her and he said, as if the thought had just occurred to him:

'To make it more amusing for Jimmy, it will be a Chinese party, and all the guests shall wear Chinese costume.'

Velda looked at him in astonishment.

'I will send your fancy-dress costumes to you tomorrow afternoon,' he said, 'and my carriage will pick you up at six-thirty.'

Velda felt there was nothing she could say.

She could only stand looking at him and her green eyes seemed to fill her whole face.

For a moment there was silence.

Then Mike Medway walked towards the door and opened it.

Feeling there was something she should say to him, but was not certain what it was, very slowly she followed him.

He did not wait for her but stepped out on deck and called to Jimmy.

He was at the bow of the Junk looking at the back of the Dragon which was her figurehead.

'Jimmy!' he called.

The boy turned and ran across the deck towards him.

'This is the most exciting ship in the world!' he exclaimed. 'When I grow up I'm going to have one just as big!'

'We shall have to see about that,' Mike Medway said. 'In the meantime, your sister will tell you that I have arranged a fireworks party especially for you, and you will be the host to all the boys with whom you will be going to School.'

'A fireworks party? Will it be here, on *The Sea Dragon*?'

'Of course!' Mike Medway said, 'and I promise you the fireworks will be the biggest and best that Hong Kong has ever seen!'

Jimmy gave a shout of sheer delight and flung his arms round Mike Medway's waist and tried to hug him.

As he did so Mike Medway looked at Velda who had joined them and saw there were tears in her eyes.

He did not say anything but took Jimmy by the hand and led him to the gangway.

'I have a lot of work to do, sending out the invitations for your party,' he said, 'and making sure the food is just as delicious as that you have enjoyed today.'

'The fireworks will be really big?' Jimmy questioned, 'and they will be ones that go up to the sky and fall down like stars?'

'There will be plenty of those,' Mike Medway promised.

They reached the gangway and Cheng was waiting there with a basket.

Mike Medway took it from him and put it into Jimmy's hand.

'Some chocolates and some of the other things you enjoyed at luncheon for your supper tonight,' he said, 'but do not make yourself sick before tomorrow!'

Jimmy clasped the basket.

'I will give some to my Chinese friends,' he said, 'and they will be able to watch the fireworks from the wharf.'

'You will find a lot of the Chinese people will do that,' Mike Medway answered.

Jimmy took the first step onto the gangway.

Then he said:

'You will not forget and sail away before tomorrow comes?'

Mike Medway laughed.

'I promise I will be here tomorrow.'

Jimmy gave a sigh of relief as if this had been a real fear.

Then, as he started to walk down the gangway, Mike Medway stood to one side so that Velda could follow him.

'I hope, Miss Armstrong,' he said, 'that you will find no difficulty in carrying out my plans.'

'I . . . am just very . . . very grateful,' Velda said.

She looked up at him wanting to plead with him not to be angry with her any more.

But already he had turned away and was walking towards the Saloon.

Quickly, because she felt she was no longer wanted, she followed Jimmy down to the quay.

When they reached it she took the basket from him.

There was no need for her to speak.

Jimmy chattered the whole way home in a wildly excited state at the idea of a fireworks party.

As he talked Velda knew that Mike Medway was in fact, being very clever, while she herself had been incredibly foolish.

Of course, if the women of Hong Kong thought he was giving a party for her, they would, as he had said, chatter about it like parakeets.

She was sure from what Bill had told her that, if he was seen dining, driving or even talking to any of the young women of the Colony, the incident would be talked about.

It would also be enlarged and exaggerated, even though there had been nothing notably peculiar about it.

She could imagine only too well how they enjoyed gossiping about *Pretty Pearl* and *Dia'mond Lil*.

Besides any of the other women who went aboard his ship.

She knew now it had been stupid of her to have imagined that there would be other guests at his dinner last night.

They would certainly have questioned why she was there.

Because she was someone new, the story would have been carried on the wind before sunrise.

'How could I have been so idiotic as not to tell him very much more sincerely how grateful I am to him for his consideration?' she chided herself.

At the same time she was perturbed by the way he addressed her so coldly.

He no longer called her Velda.

'I insulted him,' she thought unhappily, 'by running away after he had given me that delicious dinner and been so understanding about Jimmy.'

When she had put Jimmy to bed, she sat on the doorstep of the little house looking out over the harbour.

She could not see the Junk, but her thoughts went out to it.

She wondered who was dining with Mike Medway tonight.

Was it somebody who had been able to amuse him far better than she had?

Someone who would not run away in a rude and ungrateful fashion?

He had kissed her out of kindness.

Of course he had, because he was sorry for her.

Because he thought of her as he thought of Jimmy, as just a child.

'How can I have been so stupid, and so uncontrolled?' she asked.

At the same time, when she thought about it, she could feel that same strange, lightning-like sensation seeping through her.

It made her feel afraid in a manner she did not understand.

She got up and went inside to shut out the lights below.

She could no longer see the harbour and the stars shining overhead, and the beauty of the night.

It hurt her, although she did not understand why.

It was difficult the next day to make Jimmy do any lessons.

So she turned the sums into fireworks and told him to count how many he wished to see let off from *The Sea Dragon*.

After breakfast Velda hurried to the Warehouse where her pupils were waiting.

She taught all ages.

They sat cross-legged on the ground as they repeated after her the words of the things she drew on the blackboard.

This morning it was as hard for her to concentrate as it had been for Jimmy.

She struggled on for two hours.

Finally she told them there would be fireworks on *The Sea Dragon* tomorrow night.

They must ask their parents if they could watch them.

The children did not shout with delight as Jimmy had done.

They merely smiled, but the excitement she could see in their eyes seemed to light up the dreary warehouse.

As she dismissed them, the majority of them put their hands into their pockets.

They took out a coin or perhaps two that their parents had given them to pay for their lessons.

There was a red tin standing on a broken chair near the door.

As the children filed past it they put the money in it.

Velda could hear the tinkle as it hit the bottom of the tin.

One or two slipped out in a shame-faced way without paying.

When she carried it back to the house she knew it contained sufficient to ensure that she and Jimmy would not go hungry tomorrow.

In fact, this was impossible.

Jimmy's basket from *The Sea Dragon* contained not only the chocolates and sweetmeats, he had enjoyed so much.

There was also a carefully wrapped duck that had already been cooked.

'How can anyone be so kind?' Velda asked herself as she put the duck on a plate.

Then she found there were small stuffed apples to go with it, as well as walnuts and special herbs.

The following day it was impossible to make Jimmy think of anything but the fireworks.

He was so excited about them that Velda began to fear that something might happen to prevent them taking place.

Or that Mike Medway might forget his promise.

Then she knew it was impossible.

At the same time she was aware that if such a catastrophe did happen, it would break Jimmy's heart.

They were, however, reassured when, soon after luncheon, there was a knock on the door.

When Jimmy ran to open it there was a man carrying two large dress-boxes.

'It's our clothes – our Chinese clothes!' Jimmy exclaimed excitedly.

Velda opened Jimmy's box first.

She found a Chinese tunic of dark emerald green with trousers of orange satin.

There was a Dragon embroidered on the back of the tunic and Jimmy was thrilled with his Chinese shoes which turned up at the toes.

He insisted on trying everything on immediately.

Because Velda told herself, Mike Medway did everything to perfection, Jimmy's clothes fitted him exactly.

She then opened her own box feeling a little nervous as to what she would find.

Mike Medway had chosen for her, and she thought he had chosen it personally, a tunic of deep rose pink satin embroidered with flowers in many colours.

It was piped at the neck and down the sides with a pale leaf green.

She knew it was almost the colour of her eyes and wondered if Mike Medway was aware of it.

The trousers were pink and over them was a straight slit-skirt which the Chinese wore on formal occasions.

This was richly embroidered with on the front and back, the same flowers as on the tunic.

She laid the clothes on the bed feeling she had never expected to possess anything so beautiful.

Also in the box she found a wreath of flowers to wear on her head.

It was in the pointed shape the Chinese women wore at Festivals and was, Velda found, exceedingly becoming.

Jimmy refused to be separated from his costume.

With difficulty Velda persuaded him not to put it on until it was time for them to dress for the party.

She changed first, knowing she would have to prevent Jimmy, once he was ready, from waiting for the carriage up on the road.

They were wearing Chinese costumes that were very different from how the poorer Chinese who lived around them dressed.

She knew if they were seen it would cause a great deal of comment.

Finally, Bill went to the top of the road to warn them of the carriage's arrival.

Then it came he called them and they hurried up the path.

They were able to leave without their neighbours being aware of what was happening.

In fact Velda thought, after what she had said yesterday and today to the children she taught, they would already be down on the wharf.

They drove down the hill in the same smart carriage that Mike Medway had fetched her in when he took her to dinner.

Velda was as excited as Jimmy.

She had taken a last glance at herself in the mirror that hung in her bedroom.

She thought that only a Geni, as she had thought him to be, could have been clever enough to dress her without her being too proud to accept his offer.

But Fancy-Dress was different.

She could give it back tomorrow.

Not even her mother would have disapproved of something that had been lent for a special occasion.

She wondered, although she was rather ashamed of her thoughts, whether Mike Medway would admire her in her Chinese garb.

She told herself, however, that it was obvious from his coldness towards her a few days ago that he was not interested in her as a woman.

She had of course, entirely misunderstood what he had said before he kissed her.

Perhaps he had been teasing her.

Perhaps she had just made a muddle of the whole episode.

Or which was far more reprehensible, she had read into what she had thought he said a great deal more than he intended.

'He must have thought me very fast and forward,' she told herself despairingly.

She wished, like so many other people before her, that she could turn back the clock.

When they reached the wharf and before the horses could come to a standstill, Jimmy was leaning out of the window.

He was exclaiming with delight at the way the Junk was decorated.

There were flags fluttering from the mast.

Bunting in the exquisite shapes that only the Chinese could achieve festooned its sides.

There were flowers everywhere on the deck.

Velda was not surprised to find that the seamen on duty were wearing Chinese native dress.

When Cheng escorted them to the Saloon they went in to find that Mike Medway was dressed as a Mandarin.

His gown, needless to say, was magnificent, and one look told Velda it was very old and valuable.

Without any formality Jimmy ran towards him to say:

'We are here! We are here! And I thought it would never happen!'

'Well, it has,' Mike Medway said, 'and do not forget that it is your party, and you will receive the guests with me.'

He turned to Velda to say:

'Good evening, Miss Armstrong, and as tonight we are behaving like the Chinese we do not shake hands, but merely bow.'

He paused a moment and continuing said:

'And now, may I welcome you to my humble ship which you honour with your presence.'

He was speaking as a Mandarin would have done and Velda gave a little laugh.

Then she went down on her knees and bent forward, until her forehead touched the ground.

Jimmy looked at her in surprise, but Mike Medway said:

'Excellent! At the same time, I do not think we can expect our guests to act their parts so skilfully.'

Velda sat back on her heels.

'I am sure they would do so, if you asked them.'

'But think how they would regret such humility tomorrow,' he replied, 'and I should be in the firing-line for months.'

Velda laughed because she knew this was true.

Then Mike Medway took Jimmy by the hand and they went out on deck to await the arrival of their first guests.

Velda knew perceptively that he wished her to remain in the background, and therefore stayed in the Saloon.

When the guests began to arrive a number of them came into the Saloon where Cheng and the Chinese boys were carrying round drinks.

The mothers of the School-boys were obviously curious to know who she was.

When she told them she was Ralph Armstrong's daughter they asked why they had not heard of her since her mother's death.

They were also curious to know where she was living in Hong Kong.

She managed to evade the more difficult questions.

It was a relief when they went out on deck to eat the delicious food which had been arranged on long tables.

Everybody helped themselves.

Velda thought there was enough food to have lasted her and Jimmy for a year.

But the boys, especially the older ones, heaped their plates with a little of everything that was available.

Finally they had what looked like pyramids of food.

Mike Medway did not speak to her and she was able to watch him moving among his guests.

He was being, she knew, so charming that every woman was captivated by him.

She could hear too the fathers of the boys saying amongst themselves that he was a 'jolly good fellow'.

She remembered her father saying in the past that most rich men were envied.

In a number of cases they were even hated by their contemporaries because they were so envious.

There was, however, something about Mike Medway, she thought, that charmed everybody to whom he talked.

Despite being so rich and powerful, they genuinely liked him.

As soon as darkness fell the fireworks began.

As Mike Medway had promised they were even better and more magnificent than the displays he had put on in the past.

At any rate, that was what everybody was saying.

Velda thought it would be impossible for a single person to produce anything so spectacular in such a short space of time.

Fireworks swept up to the sky to cascade down in a spray of red, green and yellow.

Fountains appeared to be coming out of the water.

After an hour of whizz-bangs and falling stars, a set-piece was lit up on another ship a little further out in the harbour.

The young boys all rushed to the side of the Junk to see it.

First came a square of white lights. Then these were joined by an inside row of red, and finally blue.

Then, in the centre, lights came on slowly, spelling out:

'*GOODNIGHT AND GOOD LUCK*
JAMES ARMSTRONG!'

There was a shout of delight as the last name went up.

Then the boys were cheering, shouting and waving.

Jimmy stood, his face crimson with excitement, and yet his eyes were a little shy.

Velda knew that Mike Medway had paid his debt to her father and no one could have done it more generously, or more completely.

Reluctantly, because it had been such a good party, the parents collected their children to take them home.

A number of them told Velda that she must come and visit them and that they would ask her and Jimmy to luncheon or tea.

'I imagine your brother will be starting School after Easter,' one of the mothers said, 'so we shall have time for the boys to be friends before Jimmy faces his first day.'

'That would be very nice for him,' Velda smiled.

At the same time, she could not help wondering if the mothers knew where she lived they would be so anxious to be friends.

Too late she thought she should have accepted the house that Mike Medway had offered her.

She had been very foolish to think there was anything wrong in his plans.

He had only been thinking of Jimmy.

Now it would be impossible for her to entertain in the neighbourhood where they lived.

Their house was little more than a coolie's shack.

She wondered if she should speak to Mike Medway and perhaps explain how she had misunderstood what he had said.

Then the last guest had said goodnight and it was obvious that he wished her to go too.

'My carriage is waiting for you,' he said to Velda, 'and I hope you have enjoyed the evening.'

'I have no . . . words to . . . express my . . . thanks,' she said softly.

She thought as she spoke that he was not listening, because he bent down to pick Jimmy up in his arms.

'Well, young man,' he said, 'were the fireworks what you wanted?'

'They were scruptious – better than any fireworks I've ever seen before!' Jimmy replied.

As if he could not find the words, he put his arms round Mike Medway's neck and hugged him.

'You are the kindest man in all the world!' he said.

He kissed his cheek.

Mike Medway laughed as he put him down on the ground.

'At least somebody appreciates me,' he said.

Velda wanted to say that she did too.

But somehow it was impossible with Cheng and the seamen on guard listening, and Jimmy still talking about the fireworks.

Mike Medway did not shake hands with her, but as she started down the gangway he said:

'Goodbye, Miss Armstrong. I am leaving tomorrow night, but I will get in touch with Jimmy when I return.'

Before she could answer he had turned away.

There was nothing she could do but follow Jimmy down to the carriage.

At last they were home.

She had undressed Jimmy and put him to bed, and folded neatly their costumes before putting them back in their boxes.

Jimmy still wanted to talk, but she shut his door and went into her own bedroom.

She had forgotten to take off the wreath from her head.

Now as she looked in the mirror she knew she looked very different from how she did ordinarily.

She wondered if Mike Medway had noticed her.

Perhaps he thought she was just a boring girl who had made a scene after he had asked her to dinner.

It must have annoyed him that she had changed his plans after he had obviously given them a great deal of consideration.

'I am a fool!' she chided herself as she looked in the mirror, 'a fool who has been offered a rainbow to Heaven, but did not know how to climb it!'

She took off the wreath.

She felt as she did so that she could hear Mike Medway's deep voice saying she was wasting her beauty.

'It must be the sort of thing he has said a thousand times to a thousand different woman!' she thought. 'What have I got to offer him when he has all the beauties in Hong Kong, Singapore and anywhere else in this part of the world doing everything he asks?'

She was not quite certain what that would be.

Undoubtedly they would be only too thrilled if he tried to kiss them.

They would not be so half-witted as to fight him off and run away.

'Perhaps, if he leaves tomorrow, I will never see him again.'

She wondered why the idea hurt her almost physically.

Because she wanted his approval and she wanted him to think her beautiful as he had once said she was, she put the wreath back on her head.

Now she looked as she had when she had gone to the party in her beautiful Chinese costume.

She knew it was far more ornate than any worn by the other women at the party.

The majority of mothers had come wearing Chinese dress because they had been asked to do so.

The fathers had worn just a tunic over their ordinary clothes and a coolie hat.

A few like Mike Medway, had borrowed a Mandarin's gown.

None of them had been as fine as his, just as Velda was sure her pink tunic with its exquisitely embroidered flowers was lovelier than any other lady's.

It suddenly struck her that to obtain such a costume so quickly Mike Medway must have borrowed it from one of his Chinese lady-friends.

She wondered if it belonged to *Pretty Pearl* or *Diamond Lil* .

Perhaps it was some exquisite Beauty that Bill and the gossips had not yet heard about.

Now there was a pain like the stab of a dagger in Velda's breast.

Then as she turned from the mirror with a little sob, she knew that she loved Mike Medway.

CHAPTER FIVE

The next day both Velda and Jimmy felt deflated.

Although they could talk about what had passed there was nothing to look forward to as there had been yesterday.

'I wish we could have fireworks every day,' Jimmy said wistfully at breakfast.

'Then you would not enjoy them as much as you did last night,' Velda said.

'I would!' Jimmy replied firmly.

He ate a little more of his breakfast before he said:

'Perhaps Mr. Medway will give me another firework party when he comes back.'

'You are not to be greedy,' Velda said automatically.

At the same time, she knew if Jimmy was looking forward to seeing Mike Medway again, so was she.

'I want to see him . . . I want to talk to him, I want to explain to him that I am . . . sorry I was so . . . stupid,' she thought.

She had the frightening feeling that when he did return he would no longer be interested in Jimmy.

That meant she would not see him and she was certain he was already bored with her.

How could he be anything else when she was so foolish?

All through the day she kept on going over what had happened the night before.

The cold way he had spoken to her, the manner in which he had turned away as they said goodbye.

She had vivid pictures of him moving amongst the guests and the small boys looking up at him adoringly.

The parents had manoeuvred themselves into a position so that he was forced to speak to them.

The Head Master of the School was obviously extremely impressed by him.

He had come into the Saloon to shake hands with Velda and say:

'I am delighted, Miss Armstrong, to know that your brother will be a pupil at my School, and of course it is through him we are having this delightful party.'

'The fireworks are always a treat for any small boy,' Velda replied.

'It is something they will remember for a very long time,' the Head Master said, 'and of course, Mr. Medway always does things in such grand style.'

He accepted another glass of champagne as he spoke.

Velda wondered if that too was a treat for him.

She had enjoyed the fireworks as they were taking place, but she found it difficult not to keep watching Mike Medway.

She did not at the time realise why she was interested in watching him.

Now that she knew she loved him she thought despairingly that it was a more foolish thing to do than anything she had done before.

To love Mike Medway was like reaching for the moon and knowing that to the man inside it, she was completely insignificant.

Yet – once – he had kissed her.

She felt herself thrill at the memory.

Then she forced herself to try to think of something else.

Every time Jimmy talked of Mike Medway, she felt her heart turn over in her breast.

It was impossible to make him talk of anything else.

The day seemed to drag by.

The children Velda taught were lethargic because they too had stayed up so late.

Jimmy was bored by his lessons and she herself felt as the day progressed that the whole world had vanished.

Only one man remained, and he seemed to dominate everything.

'I love him!' she told the dhows in the harbour.

'I love him!' she called to the gulls overhead as they glided out to sea.

'I love him!' she murmured to the sampans as they rocked near the shore.

She saw a British warship and it made Mike Medway seem nearer to her because he was British.

'I cannot go on like this!' she said angrily to herself.

She went into the house slamming the door behind her.

When Jimmy came in from playing with his Chinese friends he said:

'Let us go down to the wharf, Velda, and see the new ship in which Mr. Medway is going to sea.'

'How do you know it is a new ship?' Velda enquired.

'Bill told me. He is going to Japan in a ship that is called *The Sea Horse*.'

Velda knew already that a great number of Mike Medway's ships were prefaced with the word 'Sea'.

There was *The Sea Dragon – The Sea Serpent, The Sea Sprite, The Sea Maiden*, and several others she had forgotten.

If *The Sea Horse* was a new one it would be very up-to-date and, she suspected, faster than those which were older.

He had, she knew, a Fleet of his own.

Yet, as she had guessed when she dined with him, *The Sea Dragon* was his home.

'I think,' she said in answer to Jimmy's request, 'it might seem as if we were pushing ourselves forward if we went to the wharf to look at *The Sea Horse*.'

She paused a moment and then went on:

'If Mr. Medway saw us he would think we were trying to come aboard.'

'I just want to see the ship,' Jimmy said sulkily. 'I am bored with playing in the yard.'

'I tell you what we will do,' Velda said. 'We will walk up towards the Peak and when we are high up, we will be able to see *The Sea Horse* below us without Mr. Medway thinking we are prying.'

Jimmy thought this was better than nothing, and they set off to walk up the steep streets which led to the Peak.

They passed the gardens of the rich residents' houses with their wonderful displays of crimson, purple and gold azaleas.

The frangipani trees with their creamy waxen temple flower blossom were in bloom.

There was a mass of flowers they could see through the gates, and by peeping over the walls.

'I would like to live in one of these houses,' Jimmy said.

Velda did not reply that it was what she would like too.

Then she knew why they were both growing discontented.

They had seen the luxury in which Mike Medway lived when they had enjoyed his hospitality.

'It was a mistake ever to become involved with him,' Velda told herself.

Yet, at the same time, she knew that her whole being cried out towards him.

Again she asked how she could have been so stupid as to run away when he had kissed her.

They climbed a little way up the Peak, then sat down to look at Victoria from a different angle.

Now the harbour lay before them, stretching over to Kowloon.

To the right they could see below them the Race-Course in *Happy Valley* which was only separated from the Chinese Cemetery by a fence of bamboos.

Below too were the water-front buildings which were vaguely Italianate in style.

Even from this height the waterfront was picturesquely Chinese.

Velda could pick out the Coolie hats moving amongst the crowds and looking like yellow mushrooms.

Gradually she started to identify the ships moored to the wharf.

It was not difficult to guess that the long, thin grey cargo-ship which was near *The Sea Dragon* was *The Sea Horse*.

'If we wave to him,' Jimmy said, 'do you think Mr. Medway will see us?'

'We are too far away, dearest,' Velda answered. 'You must just send him your wishes for Good Luck on his journey, and hope he is aware of it.'

'I would rather talk to him,' Jimmy replied.

Velda thought that was what she would like too.

Then she was ashamed of herself for being obsessed by a man who was not interested in her.

She changed the subject and told Jimmy a Fairy-Story.

It was a story she made exciting with Knights pursuing a dangerous Dragon.

As they reached home she thought that even in her stories she could not escape from Mike Medway.

Jimmy was tired from the long walk.

She offered him one of the sweetmeats left in the basket.

He ate some for his tea, then reluctantly went to find his Chinese friends.

'Soon he will have the boys at School to play with,' Velda told herself, 'and they will ask him to their homes so that he will have English friends.'

'And what about you?' her brain asked her.

It was a question she did not want to answer.

She forced herself to occupy her mind by washing Jimmy's socks and a pair of short trousers.

He got very dirty when he was playing in the yard.

As she hung his things out on the line to dry she found herself looking down into the harbour.

In a few hours' time Mike Medway would be leaving Hong Kong and on his way to Japan.

She tried not to wonder when he would be back.

He had done what was expected of him and had paid his debt to her father.

Doubtless there would be some exquisite Japanese girl waiting for him in Tokyo.

The idea hurt her so much that it was a relief when Bill appeared.

'Them were fine Foireworks last night, Miss Velda!' he commented.

'You enjoyed them?' Velda asked knowing he had been down on the wharf.

'Oi thinks they be th' best as 'as ever been let 'orf,' Bill replied.

'It was a wonderful party for Jimmy!'

'Ye can bet everybody'll be talkin' about it in Hong Kong ter-day,' Bill said, 'an' Oi 'ears already they're sayin' t'was good of 'im to 'ave all 'em boys aboard, considerin' 'e's got no children of 'is own.'

'It must be very sad for him not to have a son!' Velda said softly.

'There's plenty as be wonderin' to who 'e's goin' to leave 'is millions when 'e dies,' Bill said speculatively.

'That will not be for many years,' Velda replied.

'Oi 'spect that's wot 'e 'opes,' Bill agreed. 'But in these 'ere waters, every man's got 'is enemies.'

'Not Mr. Medway,' Velda replied. 'I was thinking last night how all the men present were saying nice things about him.'

'But they be English!' Bill pointed out. 'There be others as ain't so complimentary.'

'What do you mean by that?' Velda enquired.

Bill was silent for a moment before he said:

'There ain't nobody as rich as Mr. Medway an' don't 'ave rivals as be jealous of 'is success.'

Velda gave a little cry.

'Now you are frightening me, and I cannot believe that Mike Medway, of all people, could be in any danger.'

She put Jimmy to bed.

After Bill had gone back to his shack in the yard, Velda found herself wondering if he knew something he had not told her.

Could it be possible that Mike Medway *was* in danger?

Could he really have enemies who wished to hurt him?

Because he was richer and more successful than they were no one would feel murderous about it!

She started to undress, then stopped.

She wanted to see Mike Medway leave Hong Kong safely in his new ship.

At least when he was at sea there would be nothing to menace him except the pirates.

But they were almost defunct, having been dealt with not only by Mike Medway but also the Royal Navy.

She had heard how successful he had been at fighting them off when they tried to board his ship.

Doubtless, he had been instrumental in sending for Naval vessels to protect the cargoes coming into the harbour.

But there was still a danger even to someone as omnipotent as Mike Medway.

Impulsively Velda went to her cupboard.

Taking a shawl which had belonged to her mother, she slipped it over her shoulders.

Then she went out of the house and walked up the rough path to the road.

There she started to walk downhill to where she knew she would be nearer to *The Sea Horse*.

She would be able to watch her departure.

She had no intention of going down to the wharf.

Just like the paths that ran down to their own house there were paths which led to many dwelling places perched on the rising ground along the harbour.

The further she walked, the larger and better-built they were.

Finally she stopped.

Then she moved off the main road and down the path which led her past several well-to-do houses to a small piece of open ground.

It was a place from which one could view the whole harbour.

There was a wooden bench under what remained of an ancient mimosa tree.

Velda sat down on the bench.

Now it was getting on towards midnight and the stars were brilliant in the sky.

The harbour was not so busy as it had been earlier in the day.

She watched a small Tug cockily towing three huge barges behind it.

Then she turned irresistibly to her left.

Now she could see quite clearly the great bulk of *The Sea Dragon*.

Then just beyond it she was able to make out the elegant lines of *The Sea Horse*.

She could sense the activity that was taking place before it was ready to put to sea.

The last of the crates it was conveying to Japan were being hoisted aboard.

It was then Velda heard voices from below.

She realised that to her left was another look-out rather like the one where she was sitting.

There were two men talking in Cantonese, and she guessed from the thickness of the first speaker's voice that he was old.

'I here,' he was saying, 'watch my son Lu Ping.'

'It late to be working,' another man said.

'What he doing velly important, means much gold,' the old man replied.

'Much gold?' his friend questioned. 'That good. Who pay much gold these days?'

The older man chuckled and it turned into a cough.

Then he said:

'Rich Dutchman trust Lu Ping. No boy swim better!'

'He swim tonight?' the other man asked. 'Why?'

The older man lowered his voice but Velda could still hear.

'Mr. Medway leave at midnight last time!'

There was silence until the other man enquired:

'You mean – last time? That why your son get much gold?'

The older man must have nodded because he continued:

'Mr. Medway always plotected when on ship.'

The older man chuckled.

'Lu Ping know that, he swim under ship, come up other side. As ship leave harbour, Mr. Medway look towards Kowloon. Lu Ping know this. He velly clever. He kill Mr. Medway, slip back into harbour no one know what happen.'

The other man made a sound of approval.

'That clever – Lu Ping swim 'way, get big gold!'

'That right,' the other man said. 'I watch if ship come back wharf, Mr. Medway dead.'

There was a note of elation in his voice which brought Velda to her senses.

She was suddenly aware of what she had overheard and what it meant.

Mike Medway was to be killed as the ship left harbour, and somehow she had to warn him.

She struggled to her feet.

As she ran up the path back towards the road she had the terrifying feeling that already it was too late.

It must be near midnight, and she would not have time to save him.

She reached the road, then started to run quicker than she had ever run in her life.

Fortunately there was no traffic and the road let to the part of the town which was near the Quayside.

Velda ran, and went on running.

She felt in terror that she could hear a clock somewhere striking midnight and she would be too late.

Yet as if she had wings on her heels, she tore on, pushing people who got in her way to one side.

Twisting and turning she ran through the crowds which increased as she drew nearer to the wharf.

Finally she came out just above where *The Lion* was moored and swept past it.

She was too breathless even to feel relief when she saw that *The Sea Horse* was still there.

As she reached it she saw that the seamen were already casting off the ropes from the bollards on the wharf.

Two men were about to unship the gangway.

She leapt onto it.

They stared at her in astonishment as she sprang onto the deck.

Passing them she looked wildly for any sign of Mike Medway.

Then she saw Cheng and rushed towards him.

'Missie Armstlong!' he exclaimed in surprise.

'Where . . . is your . . . master?' she asked in a voice that was so breathless it was almost incoherent.

Cheng did not answer, he merely turned to open the door which led into the covered part of the ship.

The Saloon, which was small and low-ceilinged was on the left.

Mike Medway was standing inside looking at some papers which he held in his hand.

He was wearing a Naval cap.

Velda realised he was just about to go out on deck and stand, as apparently he always did, looking out at Kowloon.

Lu Ping would already be there, waiting to kill him.

Mike Medway looked up, then stared at her in disbelief.

'Velda!' he exclaimed, 'what are you doing here?'

'I . . . I have . . . come to . . . warn you,' Velda gasped. 'Y.you are to be . . . killed as . . . you leave . . . I . . . I was . . . so . . . afraid I . . . would not . . . get here . . . in t.time . . .!'

Her voice seemed to crack as she spoke.

Because she had run so fast and it was hard to breathe, she staggered.

Mike Medway reached out and manoeuvred her gently down into an armchair.

'Now, what is all this about?' he asked. 'Who is going to kill me, and how are you aware of it?'

'I . . . I heard two men . . . t.talking . . .'

'Where?'

'On the . . . look-out . . . on the . . . Kingston . . . Road.'

'Why were you there?'

'I . . . I went to . . . see you . . . l.leaving the . . . harbour.'

She gasped for breath.

Her breasts were heaving beneath the cotton gown she was wearing.

Mike Medway walked to the side of the Saloon, poured some water into a glass and brought it back to her.

'Drink this!' he commanded. 'There is no hurry. I am here, and listening to everything you have to say.'

'I . . . I thought . . . I would . . . never reach . . . you!' Velda murmured.

'But you have, and now go on with your story. You heard two men talking and they said that somebody was going to kill me?'

'It . . . is the . . . son of the . . . older man . . . who is called . . . Lu Ping . . . he is . . . being paid . . . he said . . . "much gold" . . . for doing . . . so.'

'By whom?'

94

'A Dutchman.'

Mike Medway's lips tightened.

'I know who it is,' he said. 'Go on!'

'Lu Ping is a . . . good . . . swimmer. He knows that . . . you always . . . stand when you . . . leave port . . . looking towards Kowloon. He intends to . . . climb up . . . the side . . . and . . . kill you!'

There was a note of horror in Velda's voice as she spoke the last words that was very moving.

Mike Medway put his hand over hers and said:

'It is all right. Now that you have informed me I shall not die – not tonight at any rate!'

'B.but . . . they . . . may . . . try again!'

'I shall be ready for them!'

Velda sipped a little of the water.

Because her hand was shaking he took the glass from her and put it down on the table.

As he did so she rose a little unsteadily to her feet saying:

'I . . . I ran fast . . . because I was . . . afraid of being . . . too late.'

'It was very brave of you,' he said, 'and now you must take a rickshaw home.'

He put his hand into his pocket as he spoke and drew out some notes which he put into her hand.

She was hardly aware he did so because she was looking at him.

She was thinking that if she had not reached *The Sea Horse* in time he would, at this moment, be lying dead.

It would be like the felling of a great oak tree or the sinking of a battleship.

How could Mike Medway, of all people, die in such an ignominious manner?

'It was very brave of you,' he said again.

He was standing in front of her, looking at her golden hair which had been blown in the wind.

Her breasts were still heaving tempestuously, and her lips were quivering as she drew in her breath.

Her large eyes were raised to his.

Without words she was pleading with him to take care of himself, praying that he would be safe on the journey that lay ahead.

There would be other dangers of which she could not warn him.

He knew everything she was thinking.

He could see it in her eyes, feel it with every breath she took.

'I will be very careful,' he promised as if she had spoken aloud.

Then, as she was unable to reply he said very quietly in a different voice:

'I want, Velda, more than I have ever wanted anything in my whole life to kiss you, but I am afraid, desperately afraid of frightening you again.'

Her eyes widened still more.

For a moment there was a light in them that was so dazzling it was as if a thousand candles had been lit within her.

Then she looked away and said in a whisper he could hardly hear:

'I. If you . . . kissed me . . . it would . . . be the most . . . wonderful thing that . . . could happen . . . to me . . . but it would be . . . wrong.'

'Wrong?' he asked. 'But, why?'

There was a little pause when he did not move.

After a few seconds Velda said:

'Because . . . you . . . you are . . . married.'

Mike Medway stared at her in sheer astonishment.

It was an answer he had never imagined he would hear; an answer that had never crossed his mind.

'Are you really saying . . .?' he began.

'Y.you vowed . . . "in sickness and . . . in health . . . until death us do . . . part".'

Velda was not certain whether she said the words, or merely heard them.

She only knew they constituted a gulf between her and Mike Medway.

It separated them as completely as if it was a yawning chasm, and there was no way of bridging it.

Then when he would have spoken, the door of the Saloon opened and Cheng said:

'All aboard, Master.'

Velda drew in her breath.

She put out her hand and laid it for a moment on Mike Medway's arm.

'God . . . go with . . . you,' she said softly.

Then before he could reply she had moved as swiftly as she had before, from the Saloon across the deck, and down the gangway.

He did not follow her.

He only stood where she had left him, staring at the door with unseeing eyes.

On the wharf, Velda stepped into the first rickshaw she saw.

She told the man where to go, then sat back and closed her eyes.

Slowly the tears began to trickle down her cheeks.

She had saved Mike Medway's life, but she had lost him.

The Sea Horse moved away from the wharf and Mike Medway walked deliberately out on deck.

He stood where he habitually stood with his back to Victoria facing Kowloon.

This ritual took place whenever he left harbour.

When he was a youth a Fortune-Teller had told him that it was a ship that would carry him into a golden future.

'The ship is today,' the Fortune-Teller had told him. 'What you are leaving is yesterday where you are going tomorrow. Always look forward, always believe that the best is yet to come.'

It was a prophesy which had echoed in his mind the first time he had left Hong Kong in his own ship carrying his own cargo.

He turned his back on Victoria because it was yesterday and looked at Kowloon because it was tomorrow.

His first expedition had been amazingly successful and so extraordinarily profitable.

After that he believed in every sign of luck to continue what had been a meteoric climb to fortune and success.

His only failure, and that was something he tried not to think about, had been his marriage.

Everything else had fallen into his hands and, as his admirers said, 'turned to gold'.

In five years, when most young men were just beginning their careers, he was already one of the most talked about men in the East.

His Fleet of ships grew bigger.

Not year by year, but month by month, then week by week.

The British soon appreciated his worth and supported him in every way they could.

His rivals, like the Dutchman, ground their teeth but found he was invincible.

He knew from what Velda had said exactly who it was that wished to kill him.

He could understand.

He was not only a 'thorn in the flesh', but he had nearly bankrupted the man in question.

He had taken over his sellers, his customers and his ships.

Now he waited for *The Sea Horse* to move a little further out into the stream.

He knew without looking down that Lu Ping was climbing silently up towards him.

If he had not been warned by Velda unarmed and unaware of his assassin, he would have been looking towards Kowloon.

He remembered he would tip his face up towards the stars.

He would feel it was their magic power that had helped him to become a star himself.

It was not exactly that he prayed in so many words.

Yet at night particularly, when he felt the ship moving beneath his feet and the purr of the engines in his ears, he felt his whole spirit was up-lifted towards something greater than himself.

It was a Power that had sustained, guided and inspired him.

He was aware of it since he first began to think for himself and know what he wanted.

He was grateful, God knows he was grateful.

And yet, there was one blot on his success.

One part of his life that had been a dismal failure but which he tried never to think about.

His marriage.

Lu Ping was moving higher and still higher.

The Sea Horse had almost reached the centre stream of the harbour.

In a few seconds the engines would accelerate and sweep forward into the future.

It was then Mike Medway acted.

He drew his pistol from his pocket and shot downwards accurately and decisively.

There was just one cry that was not heard by anybody else on board, and a faint splash in the water.

Then there was silence.

Mike Medway looked ahead towards Kowloon.

As he had told Velda, he would not die tonight.

CHAPTER SIX

Mike Medway stood on deck until *The Sea Horse* had negotiated the small islands before reaching the open sea.

Then he went below to his cabin.

When he was undressed and in bed, what Velda had said seemed to seep over him like a tidal wave.

Could it be possible, he asked himself, that any woman would think it wrong for him to kiss her because he was married?

The answer was it was exactly what Velda thought.

Because he was so experienced with women he could understand how for her a married man was a creature apart.

He reasoned that because her father and mother had been so happy together love was something sacred.

He had known after he had kissed her and offered her a home that she was bewildered and at the same time shocked at the idea.

He thought he was being very clever in making her aware of him in a more subtle manner.

He had to erase the impression he had created in her mind when he suggested that they would be very happy together.

Then he had known to do that he had to appear in a very different guise.

He had therefore deliberately spoken to her in a cold voice.

He had appeared indifferent to her appearance and at the party he had ignored her.

He had thought when she left that she looked a little disappointed and had glanced at him apprehensively.

It was as if she was afraid he was angry with her.

But when she had come to him tonight breathless and terrified that she would not be able to save him, he had known that he had won his battle!

She loved him!

It was what he wanted, and what he had been determined to get.

Yet, in one word, she had shattered his whole satisfaction of his achievement.

Married!

He could hear the word being repeated and repeated in his mind.

He could hear Velda's voice whispering his marriage vow.

It was, in fact, many years since it had happened and quite a number since he had thought of that moment.

He had put the wedding-ring on Irene's finger feeling excited that he was marrying one of the most beautiful girls he had ever seen.

He had thought – and it was impossible not to think it – that she would further his career.

He had been ambitious ever since he was a small child.

Both his father and mother had told him that because he was their son, and because they could have no more children, they expected great things of him.

They wanted him to be a man whom everybody respected and admired.

His father already owned two ships which were working in the East.

They brought him in quite a considerable income every year.

He had also inherited money from the generations before him besides the large Queen Anne house in which they lived.

It was both comfortable and impressive.

Long before he went to School, Michael, as he was then called, was aware that much more was expected of him.

His horizons must therefore be wider than the two-thousand acres of good Oxfordshire soil.

He travelled with his father to the East and it was at Singapore that Captain Ralph Armstrong saved his life.

It was this voyage which told him his future lay in the Indian Ocean.

He had left Oxford and his father was ready to launch him into a new world.

It was a world in which there were ships and cargoes with great fortunes to be made from them.

Then Michael Medway met Lady Irene Wood.

Her father was the Earl of Underwood, a neighbour who lived only a few miles away.

Michael met Lady Irene at the local Hunt Ball and thought she was the most beautiful girl he had ever seen.

Afterwards he knew he should have thought it was strange that the Earl favoured his suit so fervently.

That the Countess smiled on him as if he was an important aristocrat.

The marriage took place very quickly after he had proposed.

In actual fact, he saw very little of his Bride-to-be before she actually became his wife.

It seemed amazing that he should have captured anyone so lovely, and before she was spoilt by the adulation of Society.

He therefore never questioned anything that had happened until they were on their honeymoon.

Then to his surprise, he found that Irene was hysterical over quite small things.

She continually complained about the discomfort or delays which were inevitable as they were travelling in France.

She also did not respond very ardently to his love-making.

She would scream at him if he argued with her or tried to persuade her to do something she did not want to do.

It was six months before Michael Medway admitted the truth.

Throughout them, every symptom she had shown on her honeymoon had been accentuated.

At last there was no doubt in his mind that his wife was mentally deranged.

Three months later Irene was taken into a Private Hospital from which she was never to emerge.

It was then, from what the Doctors told him, he was aware that the Earl and his wife had known all along of their daughter's abnormality.

The Earl financially was in dire straits and desperately in need of money.

What could be more fortunate than that the son of his very rich neighbour should woo his daughter Irene?

'I was a greenhorn and a fool who did not use his brain!' Michael Medway told himself.

He had called at the Hospital as a duty.

He had been confronted with a wild-eyed creature who did not recognise him.

It was then he left England and went East.

Because he knew the only way to forget what he was suffering was to work, he threw himself into the business of trading.

Within a year the two ships he had received as a gift from his father became a small Fleet.

This grew greater, more important and more valuable every year.

He was young and he wanted to forget.

At every port at which he called he surrounded himself with all the most amusing people.

Englishmen in Hong Kong and Singapore welcomed him with open arms and so did the women.

His looks beguiled those that were social and his money enthralled those who sold themselves to the highest bidder.

The Important and more distinguished Chinamen and Singalese, Malays and Indians all became his friends.

As the years passed his parties, which were certainly more amusing, more outrageous and more expensive than anybody else's, became legendary.

Because he was just and kind to those who served him on his ships, they gave him their loyalties and their affection.

'Mike Medway' as he was known East of Suez gradually became a god-like figure.

He was welcome wherever he went, from Government House to the Chinese on the quayside.

Of course he enjoyed every moment of it!

He gained what he wanted, and was acclaimed as the great man in a dozen different countries.

There was only one black spot; one dark cupboard of his mind on which he shut the door.

His marriage!

Now in the darkness of his cabin it all came back to him.

The horror he had felt when Irene raged at him or screamed until the noise deafened his ears.

He had fought fiercely against the truth.

Finally he was forced to face the fact that he could do nothing to help or cure her.

Looking back, he could still feel the agony of his decision to put her into a special Hospital.

He remembered leaving the house when she was raging at him and walking through the gardens and woods.

He tried to think clearly.

He tried to make a decision he knew was too big for him to make alone.

At last, because he hated the humiliation of it, he went to see Irene's parents.

It was a shock to know as he spoke to them that they were already aware of what he was trying to tell them.

They had known from the very beginning and had deceived and trapped him.

He had felt like raging at them.

Instead the self-control which was to be characteristic of him in the future took over.

He spoke quietly and coldly.

He had told them the truth, not gently as he had intended, but bluntly and harshly.

Afterwards he left the Earl's ancestral home, never to return.

He had settled his father-in-law's bills when he married and it had cost him a great deal of money.

He told himself when he went abroad that he owed them nothing.

He hoped he would never have to speak to them again.

His own father and mother were devastated.

Like him they had been deceived into thinking it was an excellent match.

Lady Irene's social standing would be an additional advantage to their son's future.

But they had been mistaken, as he had.

Although he had no wish to do so, he found himself blaming them.

They should have known, being near neighbours, exactly what the position was.

However, he told himself when he went East that recriminations would get him nowhere.

As the Fortune-Teller had foretold he had to forget the past.

He must not look back at yesterday but forward – the future was tomorrow.

It was almost true to say that, in the last few years, he had really succeeded in forgetting Irene's existence.

There were a great number of women ready to help him to do so.

Some of them were English, the majority Chinese, Malay or Indian.

They were invariably beautiful and occasionally amusing.

He asked very little of a woman except that she should attract him as a woman and her body should be that of a goddess.

He paid generously for his pleasures and could well afford to do so.

Although some women wept as he passed out of their lives, more of them were deeply grateful to have known him.

As the Chinese said, they were honoured by his attentions.

Yet now, like the Sword of Damocles hanging over him when he least expected it, Velda had brought back the horror of his marriage.

He knew when he thought about her that he had been mistaken so far as she was concerned, from the very beginning.

She had stunned him with her beauty.

He had been sure it was only a question of time before she fell into his arms as every other woman had done.

He had kissed her.

He had felt the softness and innocence of her lips, and had experienced an entirely different sensation from anything he had known before.

He could not explain it to himself, but it was there.

He had known then he not only desired Velda as he had desired so many other women, but he also wanted her.

He wanted her close to him, he wanted to talk to her.

He wanted to listen to her soft voice saying things that were unusual and which in consequence intrigued him.

Looking back, if he was honest, he had to admit that he seldom talked to women except about love.

Their opinions were banal and not particularly interesting.

But Velda had fascinated him from the very moment she had come to ask him to sponsor her brother.

Because she was so poor, so threadbare, so under-fed, it had seemed quite natural for him to dress her, house her and love her.

She had run away from him.

It was then he vowed that she would be his.

He therefore deliberately, using his intelligence, planned his campaign as to how he would capture her.

He had known, when she had run into his Saloon with her fair hair curling round her forehead, her eyes filled with fear in case she was too late, that he had won.

Her perfectly curved breasts had been heaving tempestuously beneath her cheap cotton gown.

She had looked lovelier then than he had ever seen her; so beautiful that she did not seem real.

She might actually have been one of the goddesses in jade, rose quartz or pink coral which stood in the cabinet in *The Sea Dragon*.

He knew when she spoke that she loved him.

He could feel it vibrating from her.

When for one moment her eyes dazzled him with a radiance that illuminated her face, she was more beautiful than any woman he had ever seen.

Then, like a bomb-shell she had reminded him of his marriage.

For a moment, because he had been stunned into an awareness of it, he had no reply.

Married!

The mere word made him shudder.

The misery of what he had suffered, the horror of his screaming wife were all there.

He was forced to face it again and admit, although he had tried to forget, that it was a reality.

It was then he had reached a decision, that he would never marry again.

He vowed on everything he held sacred that never again would he be trapped by the Church and God into a travesty of what they called the 'Sacrament of Marriage'.

It was nearly dawn before Mike Medway came to a decision.

Velda was there, he wanted her, his body cried out for her.

But his brain told him, as it had before, that marriage was not for him.

There were millions of women in the world.

He would forget Velda and the sooner the better.

He slept for a few hours, then rose.

Anybody who knew him well would have seen that there was an expression on his face that had not been there before.

His grey eyes were hard and cold and his lips were set in a tight line.

There was a strange, defiant note in his voice.

Inevitably it took time to reach Tokyo.

It was a City which waited for him eagerly because he had had a great deal to do with the creation of it.

Until 1868 Tokyo had not been the Capital of Japan.

Ebo as the town was then called, consisted of primitive dwellings and was full of similar customs.

The transport had not changed since the MIddle Ages.

It was Mike Medway who had seen the possibilities of Japan keeping pace with the progress of Industry as it had developed in other parts of the East.

It was he who had helped the Japanese to adopt what was an entirely new civilisation at a moment's notice.

He had advised them who to turn to for help in the creation of their railways, their buildings and their ships.

Because they had followed his advice, their quick development had been like a miracle which was acknowledged both in the East and in the West.

When Mike Medway arrived there were a number of Dignitaries to welcome him.

There was also an even larger number of Merchants who wished to consult him.

The first two days while his cargo was unloaded he hardly had time to breathe.

Then when he could put on one side the unceasing questions of those who wished to 'pick his brains', *Kuchi-nada-hime* was waiting.

110

She was undoubtedly the most beautiful Geisha in the whole of Tokyo.

She lived up to her name, which meant 'Wondrous-Inada-Princess'.

She was waiting for him in her pretty house.

It had a green-tiled roof which stood in an exquisite garden outside the hastily-built City wall.

He thought as she hurried to greet him that nobody could be lovelier.

Except for one person – his heart told him.

He did not wish to listen.

Kushi as he called her, drew him down onto the soft cushions.

He took from his pocket the present he had brought her.

He had actually purchased it some time ago and only remembered its existence when they were steaming into port.

It was a necklace of jade and pearls with a beautifully carved pendant suspended from it.

Kushi held it in her long-nailed fingers exclaiming with delight.

She touched the floor with her forehead in gratitude before she melted into his arms.

It was very much later before Mike Medway left the little house with the green roof.

He told himself that no man could ask for anything more satisfactory, more subtle, enchanting and exotic.

Yet, as he drove back into the City, he knew that he lied.

There was a great deal for him to do, and a great many contracts to discuss and sign.

Almost despite himself he hurried his interviews which was always a difficult thing to do in the East.

He signed contracts without extracting, as he usually did, the very last cent of profit from those who were buying.

He also paid more than he intended to those who were selling.

It was then he admitted to himself that he wanted to get back to Hong Kong.

It was not easy because there were official functions at which he was the Guest of Honour.

Then there was an audience with the Emperor Mutsuhito that could not be ignored.

'There is no hurry. I am here to work and, when I do return to Hong Kong, I will not see Velda.'

He repeated this to himself over and over again as if by talking he could control the instincts of his heart.

In fact, it was his heart that gave him the most trouble.

It was something he had ignored in previous years and it had not intruded upon him in any way.

As long as his body was satisfied and his brain was working clearly, he asked for nothing more.

And yet, now, that obscure, tiresome organ which he had never really believed existed was throbbing within him and being persistently annoying.

There was no other word for it.

It annoyed him to be reminded of Velda when he looked at *Kushi*.

It infuriated him that he should remember the softness of her voice when a Geisha was fawning on him.

'Velda is only one woman,' he argued, 'and there are hundreds here who are just as desirable and there are hundreds here in Singapore, Calcutta, Bali and Batavia.'

But it was no use.

Whenever he went to bed and tried to sleep, he could see two gold-flecked green eyes looking at him.

Sometimes he saw the fear in them.

At other times they dazzled him and sparkled like the stars.

'Dammit, I am being haunted!' he said angrily one night.

He had gone to the shutters of his room to pull them back and look up at the sky.

There was a moon throwing its light over the roofs, turning the new Tokyo into an enchanted City.

'There is so much for me to do here,' Mike Medway said.

He had thought of half-a-dozen innovations he intended to suggest to the Japanese.

He knew how much they would appreciate them.

Because of the necessity of keeping pace with the world after a late start, the Japanese were imitators, rather than creators.

Mike Medway was trying to make them understand that they must seek new ideas, encourage new inventions.

There was so much to be done.

So many ways in which they could make a fortune for him as well as one for themselves.

'I will stay here for at least a month!' he told himself.

But when morning came there was a restless feeling within him which told him he had to hurry home.

Why? For what?

He had already decided that if he saw Velda, he would behave formally towards her, speaking only of Jimmy.

But that tiresome instrument the heart was beating again.

It told him that however much he tried to prevaricate he had to return to Hong Kong.

Finally, to keep everybody happy, especially *Kushi* he gave one of his fantastic parties.

He chose the largest and most important Geisha House in Tokyo in which to give it.

The Geishas came from inside and outside the City.

They were as beautiful as the almond blossom which decorated the rooms.

His friends the great Merchants, the High Officials and the Dignitaries each lent some of their precious pictures to be hung on the walls.

Mike Medway ordered all the most expensive and delicious dishes to eat.

There were also French and German wines to drink besides *Sake* which everybody expected.

Officers from every ship in the harbour were invited.

The young Lieutenants were wide-eyes with excitement.

They had never expected to be privileged enough to attend one of Mike Medway's famous parties.

It was as if he was driven by some strange urge within himself to exceed every other party he had ever given.

There were expensive presents for all the women, and amusing mementoes for the men.

Kushi looked like her name-sake – 'Wondrous-Inada-Princess'.

Her *Kimono* which Mike Medway had bought for her was exquisitely embroidered with silks intermixed with pearls, emeralds and rubies.

There were diamonds in her hair and hanging from her ears.

She wore two huge emerald rings on the first finger of each hand.

Because she was his, Mike Medway knew that every man in the room was envying him because she was so lovely.

There were dancers who portrayed eroticism in mime, and music which made a man feel the blood pulsating in his temples.

The party went on until the sun was rising in the sky.

Everybody said it was the most marvellous party they had ever attended, and one they would never forget.

Only as Mike Medway boarded *The Sea Horse* did he admit he was glad that it was all over and he wanted to go home.

Home?

Yes, home to Hong Kong to *The Sea Dragon* his treasures and his comforts.

'And what else?' asked the gulls as they rose in front of the bow.

'What else?' asked the waves as they slapped against the sides of *The Sea Horse*.

It seemed to Mike Medway that the passage home took an immeasurably long time.

Actually the Captain kept telling him they were having a record run and had reached a greater speed than they had ever achieved in the past.

Only as they steamed through the islands and up towards Hong Kong did Mike Medway have a feeling of relief he had no wish to put into words.

They notified their arrival to *The Sea Dragon* by the semaphore stations.

The great Junk had therefore moved into the wharf which it always used.

The space beside it was waiting for *The Sea Horse*.

They reached Victoria late in the afternoon.

The sun was still shining and turning the water in the harbour to gold.

It was almost as if the whole City was awaiting his return.

The wharf was crowded with the usual collection of coolies, children, rickshaw-boys, blind musicians and pedlars.

Mike Medway was not surprised when they cheered as *The Sea Horse* steamed slowly into position.

The Sea Dragon welcomed them with klaxons from the Bridge.

Mike Medway's personal flag was run up the mast.

'A record, Master!' the Captain was saying excitedly. 'We travel two hour quicker than we ever do before.'

'Well done!' Mike Medway exclaimed.

The Chinese crew who already knew of it were grinning with delight.

They knew they would receive a promised bonus from Mike Medway for the achievement.

He had also promised them a celebration dinner aboard.

He climbed down onto the wharf and walked towards *The Sea Dragon*.

A cheer went up from those who were watching him.

They welcomed him home, both in Cantonese and in English.

A woman of unknown nationality pressed a flower into his hand.

Chinese children, ragged but smiling, danced along in front of him saying:

'Firework! Make big fire-work?'

There was another cheer as he walked up the gang-plank of *The Sea Dragon*.

He turned to wave to the shouting children.

Cheng went ahead of him to open the door into the Saloon.

He had not gone with him to Tokyo.

'Welcome home, Master!'

116

'It is good to be back,' Mike Medway replied. 'Is everything all right?'

'Evlything, Master. Old sailor wish see you . . .'

'Old sailor?' Mike Medway questioned sharply.

'Bill, Master. Fliend Missie Armstlong.'

'What does he want?' Mike Medway asked.

He told himself the one person he did not want to be reminded of at the moment was Miss Armstrong.

He had come back determined not to see or contact her.

Yet now, Bill Dowd, who he knew looked after her, was here waiting to see him.

If he had any sense he would send him away.

He would make it quite clear that there was no reason for there to be any communication between him and Miss Armstrong, unless it concerned Jimmy.

He had told the Head Master he would be responsible for the boy.

Unless he was to involve himself with Jimmy's sister which was something he did not wish to do, there was nothing to discuss.

Then why was the man here?

Cheng was waiting.

It was impossible to assuage his curiosity without seeing Bill Dowd.

'I have just arrived after a long voyage!' he said. 'I am tired, and I need a drink!'

'It leady, Master,' Cheng said.

He poured a glass of champagne from an open bottle that was in the wine-cooler in a corner of the Saloon.

He offered it to Mike Medway on a silver salver.

Then he withdrew, but only as far as the door.

Deliberately slowly because he was exercising his authority not over Cheng, but over himself, Mike Medway sipped his champagne.

It was cool and refreshing.

But for some reason he did not understand he could not taste it.

It annoyed him that Cheng was standing waiting.

He obviously thought he must see Bill Dowd.

Mike Medway put down his glass and said irritably:

'Very well then, show him in! God knows, I never have a moment to myself!'

Cheng disappeared and Mike Medway drank what was left in his glass.

He was wondering, and it annoyed him that he should do so, why Bill Dowd had come to see him.

The door opened again.

'Bill fliend Missie Armstlong,' Cheng announced unnecessarily.

The old sailor with his wooden leg and supporting himself with a stick came hobbling into the cabin.

Mike Medway, seated at his desk, watched his approach.

Then he said, still in a somewhat irritated voice:

'Well? What is it?'

Bill Dowd saluted him.

'Oi thinks ye'd want t'know, Sir, that Miss Velda's very ill!'

Mike Medway stiffened.

'Ill!' he exclaimed. 'What is wrong with her?'

'Don't know, Sir. Doctor's very worried. 'E finks 'er might die!'

'I – I do not believe it!' Mike Medway exclaimed. 'What has happened?'

''Twere loik this, Sir,' Bill Dowd began. 'A'ter ye went away, Miss Velda gets a letter from that there 'Ead Master at th' School as Master Jimmy's goin' to.'

'A letter? What did he say to her?'

118

"Twas a list, Sir of th' uniform young Master Jimmy's got t'ave when 'e goes there.'

Mike Medway stared at him.

'Uniform!' he said almost beneath his breath.

It was something he had forgotten; something he had never taken into account.

'Clothes is expensive, Sir,' Bill was saying, 'so Miss Velda was a-worryin' an' starvin' 'erself a-wonderin' 'ow to pay for 'em.'

'Starving herself?'

Mike Medway almost shouted the words.

'Aye, Sir. 'Er's bin eatin' very little an' spendin' only on food fer Master Jimmy.'

Mike Medway pressed his lips together.

'How,' he asked himself silently, 'could I have forgotten that all Schools of importance expect their pupils to wear uniform?'

'Oi thinks,' Bill Dowd went on, ''Twas because 'er were so thin Miss Velda picks up th' fever from one o'em children 'er's bin teachin'.'

There was a pause.

'She has a fever!' Mike Medway said at last, as if he would confirm what Bill Dowd had told him.

''Er's got worse an' worse,' Bill answered. 'Miss Velda's be in a coma. Oi've bin lookin' a'ter Master Jimmy meself 'til ye comes back.'

'And you say – the Doctor thinks she will not – live?'

Bill Dowd made a helpless gesture with his hands.

'Oi could only get a young Chinaman, Sir. Others are expensive, an' want money afore they'll see th' patient.'

Mike Medway got to his feet.

He passed Bill Dowd and went to the door to open it.

119

Cheng was outside with the Captain and two other officers waiting to see him.

It was then Mike Medway began to give orders in a voice that was clear and crisp.

They knew as they listened that he wanted a number of things done and done immediately.

CHAPTER SEVEN

Mike Medway opened the cabin door very quietly.

The curtains were drawn over the portholes, but the sunshine still percolated through in golden rays.

A Nurse rose from the side of the large bed and walked towards him.

'How is she?' he asked in a low voice.

'Have a good night, Mr. Medway,' the Nurse replied. 'Little better this morning.'

She spoke good English, but with a Cantonese accent.

She was Chinese and had been trained in the British Hospital.

Nearly middle-aged, she was the most experienced Nurse they could provide.

Mike Medway looked towards the bed. Then he said:

'Is Dr. Wang coming again today?'

The Nurse smiled.

'Yes, Mr. Medway. Dr. Wang velly pleased yesterday. All due, he say to Chinese medicine.'

Mike Medway smiled.

He knew that Nurse Lo Nu's loyalty was divided.

There was her allegiance to what she had learnt in the British Hospital and to what, as a Chinese, she had known since childhood was efficacious when one was ill.

'Miss Velda taking Ginseng,' she volunteered as Mike Medway did not speak. 'Velly old, velly revered medicine among Chinese people.'

Mike Medway knew that this was true.

He had learnt that even in the sampans the poorest families saved up so that they could purchase a Ginseng root.

It was a medicine that had been used in China since the Middle Ages, and gave everybody who took it strength and endurance.

It had been discovered centuries ago by travellers.

They found it enabled them to complete their long journeys quicker, and without dying from exhaustion.

He did not say any more, but moved across the cabin to the bed.

Tactfully Lo Nu withdrew and he was alone with Velda.

He looked down at her, trying desperately to see any evidence to assure him she was really better.

When he had seen her lying in her bed in the small poverty-stricken house, he had thought for one terrifying moment that she was dead.

Her face was as white as the pillow on which she was lying.

She was so thin that she seemed ethereal and hardly human.

Her eyes were closed and she was very still.

It swept through his mind that it was only a question of minutes before they covered her face.

Then, almost as if he called on the Power in which he believed and to which he had always turned in every extremity, he swore she should live.

Only Mike Medway could have procured so quickly the best-known Chinese Doctor in the whole of Hong Kong.

He was a busy man and very conscious of his own importance.

But he came immediately in the carriage that Mike Medway sent for him.

From the moment he looked down at Velda, still and silent in the small bed, he and Mike Medway knew exactly what they must do.

Carefully, as if they were moving a delicate piece of white jade, Velda was carried out of the small house and up the rough path.

She was set down very gently on the back seat in one of Mike Medway's carriages.

Then she was conveyed to the Wharf.

She never stirred as she was taken aboard *The Sea Dragon*.

She was placed in the Master Cabin which Mike Medway had built and decorated entirely for himself.

With the help of Dr. Wang they obtained the services of Nurse Lo Nu from the British Hospital and another Nurse who always attended to his special patients.

For three nights and days Dr. Wang hardly left Velda's side.

To save him from coming to them, many of his other patients came to *The Sea Dragon*.

Many more, who were not so desperately ill had to wait until he could attend to them.

He only had to ask for what he wanted and Mike Medway provided it.

The crisis passed and the two men knew that Velda would live!

They were as delighted as if they had stamped out a plague or found the cure for consumption.

'I can never be sufficiently grateful,' Mike Medway said to Dr. Wang. 'If there is anything you require for yourself or your patients you have only to ask.'

'You are very gracious, Honoured Sir,' Dr. Wang replied.

Mike Medway knew by the glint in his eyes that he could not have rewarded him more generously.

It was only when Dr. Wang allowed it that *The Sea Dragon* moved away from the wharf.

They proceeded through the harbour towards one of the small islands which were uninhabited.

While all this was happening, Jimmy had not been forgotten.

Mike Medway had brought him abroad.

He found a young English student to look after him and give him lessons in Velda's place.

He was a nice young man who was thrilled at the chance of meeting Mike Medway.

He was as fascinated by *The Sea Dragon* as Jimmy was.

Looking down at Velda in the quietness of his cabin Mike Medway asked himself how it was possible for her to go on sleeping for so long.

Why she was not aware of how much he wanted her to come back to life and to him.

Dr. Wang assured him that it was only a question of time.

It was a mistake to hurry the healing process of sleep.

'She is no longer in a coma,' he said, 'she is asleep. When Winter pass come Spring.'

Mike Medway knew exactly what he meant.

At the same time, he wanted to see the Spring in Velda's green gold eyes and hear it in the softness of her voice.

'Get well, get well quickly!' he urged her silently.

He felt the Power within him flowing into her.

He wanted to bend forward and kiss her back into awareness.

But he knew it was something he must not do.

Finally with a little sigh, he turned away and walked across the cabin to the door.

Then he turned and looked back.

He thought Velda's golden hair on the pillow rivalled the sunshine seeping through the curtains.

Outside the green of the water would be the colour of her eyes.

'Get well because I want you!' he said in his heart.

He went from the cabin closing the door very quietly behind him.

Velda moved and turned her face to one side.

Instantly there was somebody beside her and a moment later she was lifted gently while a glass was held to her lips.

It was something sweet that she had tasted before.

She drank, first a sip, then a little more, until the glass was half empty.

Then as she was set down she opened her eyes.

She thought she must be back in her bedroom in the house in the country.

Then she knew the ceiling was not the same and she was somewhere strange.

'Where . . . am I?'

It was an effort to speak and her voice did not sound like her own.

A Chinese voice with a lilt in it replied:

'You safe, velly nice place, go sleep.'

She wondered who the Chinese was who was talking to her.

Then there were fingers on her forehead, moving very gently.

She thought about them and felt they were hypnotic.

Then she slipped back into the darkness from which she had come.

Velda awoke and thought she had been sleeping for a long time.

Now it must be day and she must get up and prepare breakfast for Jimmy.

She opened her eyes and saw not Jimmy, but a face that had been in her dreams.

Although she was not aware of it there was a sudden light in her eyes and her lips parted.

'I . . . I was . . . thinking . . . of . . . you.'

'You are awake,' Mike Medway exclaimed. 'You are awake, Velda!'

'Have I . . . been . . . asleep for a . . . long . . . time?'

'A very long time,' he replied.

'But . . . you are . . . back! You . . . went away.'

It was difficult to speak, and the words seemed to be spoken a little jerkily.

'I am back, I am here,' Mike Medway said, 'and now you must hurry and get well because there is so much I want to talk to you about.'

She felt his hand cover hers and the strength of his fingers.

'You are . . . back,' she said as if it was all that mattered, and fell asleep.

'How did I get . . . here? How is it . . . possible that I am . . . in *The Sea Dragon?*'

The questions seemed to pour from Velda's lips and Mike Medway, who was sitting beside her bed smiled.

'I have been waiting to tell you all about it.'

Velda smiled.

'I knew that was what . . . you meant to do . . . because Nurse was so . . . careful not to . . . answer the questions I . . . asked her.'

She paused and took a deep breath before she went on:

'She said . . . Mr. Medway would tell me . . . what I . . . wanted to know.'

'She was obeying my instructions,' Mike Medway said. 'Why should she have all the fun of waking the "Sleeping Beauty"?'

'Is . . . that what . . . I have been?'

'For nearly two weeks.'

'Two weeks? I . . . I do not . . . believe it!'

She wrinkled her brow.

'I remember feeling very ill and getting into bed because I could . . . hardly stand. Then there was only . . . darkness.'

Before Mike Medway could answer she gave a little cry.

'Jimmy! What has . . . happened to . . . Jimmy?'

'He is quite all right,' he said soothingly, 'Bill looked after him until I arrived back in Hong Kong, then I brought him aboard.'

He paused before he said:

'I think it is very important you should get well quickly and come to see what is happening to him.'

'Oh . . . is there . . . anything . . . wrong?' Velda asked fearfully.

'Not really, but I am worrying about Jimmy. He has taken over my Junk! Unless you exert a stable influence over him it will be impossible for him not to become abominably spoilt!'

'Spoilt?' Velda said in a horrified tone.

Then she realised that Mike Medway's eyes were twinkling, and that he was teasing her.

'Jimmy has captivated my crew,' he said. 'They spend their whole time playing with him, carving toys as only the Chinese can, to please him.'

Velda gave a little laugh and he went on:

The Captain is teaching him Arithmetic far more effectively that you could ever do.'

He smiled at her then went on:

'Jimmy now thinks in knots and fathoms and is determined, whether I allow it or not, to steer *The Sea Dragon* as soon as we put to sea.'

'You must not let him be a nuisance,' Velda said.

'The only difficulty is,' Mike Medway replied, 'that I find him irresistible. He is the most enchanting little boy I have ever met. I only hope that one day I have a son like him.'

He saw Velda's eyes widen.

There was a faint flush on her cheeks as she said quickly:

'I am sure it is . . . all your . . . fault for . . . spoiling him, and you must be . . . very strict if he does not . . . behave . . . himself.'

'I think that is something you should come back to do,' Mike Medway remarked.

'I am sure that in a subtle way you are trying to force me into making an effort,' Velda said perceptively.

'I can see that you are too clever for me to deceive you,' Mike Medway laughed, 'and therefore I will say it in plain English – I want you well and I want you with me – there is a great deal for us to do.'

She longed to ask what that was, then she felt shy.

It was only yesterday that she realised she was occupying the Master Cabin in *The Sea Dragon*.

She had literally turned Mike Medway out of his own bed.

How could this have happened?

She had learnt from the Nurses that she had caught a tropical fever that was very dangerous.

She also knew that it was Dr. Wang who had saved her life.

She thought secretly that it was really Mike Medway who had done that.

But she had not been brave enough yet to ask him if that was the truth.

Now as he put out his hand she placed hers into it.

'You are still far too thin,' he remarked as he looked down at her fingers.

'If I eat everything the Nurses bring me, I will soon be too fat to walk up Kingston Hill!'

'That is something you will never do again!' he said.

She looked at him in surprise, then she asked:

'You have . . . not done . . . anything with our . . . house?'

'I have given it to Bill Dowd,' Mike Medway said, 'and a pension to enable him to live there.'

Velda looked at him in consternation.

'But . . . what about . . . Jimmy and . . . me?'

'That is something about which I am going to talk to you later,' he said, 'and now I am going to leave you to rest. Jimmy can come to see you as soon as you are awake.'

'I am tired of sleeping,' Velda said almost petulantly, 'and I want to see Jimmy.'

'And I want you up and with us,' Mike Medway said, 'so for the moment you have to obey orders.'

He rose to his feet.

Then, as Velda looked up at him towering above her, he said:

'Hurry! You are now wasting time, as you wasted your beauty.'

Before she could think of a reply he had gone.

Jimmy had a great deal to say.

'It's very exciting here on *The Sea Dragon*, Velda! And what do you think? Now that we have moved to an island so that you can have peace and quiet, I have been riding.'

'Riding!' Velda exclaimed.

'Uncle Mike . . .' Jimmy began.

'*Uncle* Mike?' Velda enquired. 'Did he tell you to call him that?'

Jimmy nodded.

'It was too difficult to keep saying "Mister Medway" and it's much easier to say "Uncle Mike".'

He looked at her to see if she was about to argue, then added:

'He's a nice Uncle, and I love him very much!'

'Go on telling me about your . . . riding,' Velda prompted.

She felt their whole life had changed without her approval, but there was nothing she could do about it.

'Uncle Mike brought several of his race-horses to the island and we exercise them every morning. It's very exciting, Velda, and he says I ride very well.'

Velda knew this was something that would have pleased her father.

He had loved riding, as he had loved doing everything else.

He had wanted his son to love horses and appreciate them, and not only because he was backing them.

'When I'm grown up,' Jimmy was saying, 'I'm going to have race-horses all of my own besides a Junk as big as *The Sea Dragon*.'

'You will have to be very clever to follow in Mr. Medway's footsteps.'

'Uncle Mike is going to help me make my fortune,' Jimmy said complacently.

It was no use saying anything, Velda thought.

It seemed as if everything was being settled without her.

The only thing she wondered was where she came into the picture.

When Jimmy left her she waited impatiently for her next visitor.

Today for the first time since she had been ill she looked in the mirror.

She was horrified to see how thin her face was, and thought perhaps Mike Medway would find her repulsive.

Her eyes seemed enormous.

When she looked down at her hands she could see how very thin her fingers had become.

The bones in her wrists were sticking out.

'I must eat and eat,' she told herself.

She remembered reading how the beautiful Empress of Russia had dieted so that she would look elegant on a horse.

Her father had voted the Empress as being the best rider in Europe but he had added laughingly:

'I understand the Emperor said that he hates thin women!'

Remembering this now, Velda wondered if Mike Medway would feel the same way.

She had always been slim, but that was a different thing from being thin and bony.

'I must eat more,' she told herself.

Then her heart leapt and she felt a sudden constriction in her throat because the door of the cabin opened and he came in.

He was smiling and looked, she thought, happy and because it was very hot he was dressed all in white.

It made him seem even larger and more overwhelming than ever.

'I am told you are very much better today – in fact, almost yourself,' he said.

'I want to get up,' Velda replied.

'That is what I wanted you to say and it is something I promise you shall do very shortly.'

He saw down on a chair beside the bed and she said:

'Jimmy has been telling me how you have been teaching him to ride and it is very, very kind of you.'

'I have enjoyed having him with me,' Mike Medway said, 'and he has the making of a fine horseman.'

'I was thinking how that would please my father.'

'And do you think he would have been pleased with you?' Mike Medway asked.

Velda looked at him enquiringly.

'How could you have been so idiotic as to starve yourself to buy Jimmy's School uniform?'

There was silence and she knew he was waiting for her answer.

'H.how . . . how do you . . . know I . . . did that?'

'Bill told me – and it made me very angry!'

Velda gave a little cry.

'Oh . . . please . . . please . . . do not be . . . angry with me. It was just that I . . . did not want to be an . . . encumbrance on you when you have . . . done so much for us . . . already.'

'So you nearly killed yourself,' he remarked. 'And if you had died, your death would have been at my door.'

'Oh, no . . . of course not . . . and I could not . . . help getting a fever!'

'If you had not been weak you would not have caught it!' he said sternly.

'Please . . . forgive me.'

She thought as she spoke that she could not bear him to be angry with her.

Because she was looking at him pleadingly he said:

'I will forgive you if you promise me never to do anything of which I would disapprove again.'

'That is a very big . . . promise!' Velda said defensively.

'It is what I want you to give,' he answered, 'and I think I deserve it after all the misery you have caused me.'

She stared at him incredulously.

Could it be possible that Mike Medway had really been perturbed because she had been so ill?

Then she thought it was not so much misery as discomfort.

He was waiting and she felt he was going to insist on her promise.

She put out her hand towards him.

'H.how can I . . . help doing anything you ask . . . when you have been so very kind . . . to Jimmy, and I have . . . even turned you . . . out of . . . your bed.'

Mike Medway smiled.

'I hope you have found it comfortable.'

'You know it is like sleeping on a cloud,' Velda replied.

She looked into his eyes.

She felt in a strange way he was trying to say something which he did not put into words.

Then he said quietly:

'I accept your promise and I know that now I have no opposition it will make it much easier for me to carry out my plans.'

'What . . . plans?' Velda asked.

He had taken her hand when she held it out to him.

Because he was touching it she felt a little thrill run through her.

Although she could not help being worried by what he was saying she felt as if her whole body was pulsating towards him.

Nothing mattered but that he was there.

'I have a plan,' he said, 'and now that you have given me your promise, it is much easier to put it into action and not have to waste words trying to explain.'

'Now you are making me very curious,' Velda complained, 'and if your plan concerns . . . me, I shall be . . . . frightened in case it . . . goes off like a . . . firework.'

She paused a moment then continued:

'I only know it has . . . happened when it is. shooting up into the sky!'

Mike Medway laughed.

'You always say the unexpected,' he said, 'and because I want to surprise you, everything will just happen and there will be nothing you can do about it.'

Her fingers tightened on his.

'Everything you . . . do is so . . . very wonderful,' she said, 'that I do not know . . . how to tell you how . . . grateful I am.'

'I have already said it would be a mistake to waste words,' Mike Medway replied, 'so please just wait and see.'

He rose as he spoke, still holding her hand in his.

Then he bent and kissed it.

Velda drew in her breath.

At the touch of his lips on her skin she felt again that same streak of lightning that she had felt when he kissed her lips.

Because she could not help herself her fingers clung to his.

'You look very lovely!' he said.

Then he was gone.

It was later in the evening.

Velda knew that Jimmy had come back from riding on the island.

Suddenly she heard the engines start up.

When Cheng came to the door to hand her tea to the Nurse who was waiting to take it from him Velda called out:

'Cheng, where are we going?'

Cheng put his head into the cabin.

'You better, Missie Armstlong!' he said. 'Evlybody happy!'

'Where are we going?' Velda asked again.

'Go back Hong Kong,' Cheng replied. 'Master give orders.'

Velda shut her eyes.

They were going back to Hong Kong.

Perhaps Mike Medway had made arrangements for her and Jimmy to move into a house.

It would be the house he had offered her originally which she had refused.

But now that Bill had taken over theirs she would be obliged to accept anything he did for her.

She had a sudden fear that, in leaving the island, she would lose Mike Medway.

It had been wonderful to be able to see him as she had for the last days at regular intervals.

Last night he had come in quite late to say goodnight before she went to sleep.

'When I am well again,' she thought, 'I want to be with him, I want to talk to him. Oh, why can we not stay here?'

She knew it was a question she could not ask him.

When he did come to see her she must apologise for having taken up so much of his time.

Her Chinese Nurses had massaged her twice a day while she had been lying in bed.

She knew how the Chinese believed that massage was very important for muscles that were limp because of inactivity.

She had walked about the cabin last night.

She had not felt in the least dizzy, nor had it been difficult to walk.

'In fact, if Mike Medway asked me to,' she told herself, 'I could dance with him!'

She wondered if that would ever happen.

Then she remembered that she had not danced for a long time.

When her father was alive and he had waltzed with her while her mother played the piano.

But there had been no piano when they had come to live in Hong Kong.

She had sometimes danced alone round the room in the little house and imagined she was at a Ball.

Now she could feel *The Sea Dragon* moving out to sea.

She wished the engines would break down and stop.

Then they would have to stay where they were.

Instead, when Mike Medway came to say goodnight, she said:

'I expect . . . you are . . . looking forward to . . . being back in . . . Hong Kong and there . . . will be a . . . lot of people . . . waiting to . . . see you.'

'I know,' he replied. 'That is why we are going to creep in very quietly at six o'clock this evening, and I hope there will not be too many "Nosey Parkers" waiting about.'

'It is impossible to keep a secret in Hong Kong,' Velda smiled.

'Perhaps, but you never know. I may surprise them!' Mike Medway replied.

He was about to leave her when she said:

'You will . . . come and say . . . goodnight to . . . me?'

'You can be sure of that,' he answered.

The sun was setting and the light coming into the cabin had a rosy hue to it as they reached the wharf.

The Sea Dragon came to a standstill and both the Nurses came into the cabin.

'We come help you dless,' Lo Nu said.

'Dress!' Velda exclaimed. 'Am I to get up?'

'Mr. Medway want you in Saloon in half-hour time.'

Velda looked at them in astonishment.

Then she felt excitedly that she was going to dine with Mike Medway.

She could think of nothing more thrilling.

The Nurses washed her and brought her some silk underclothes she had never seen before.

The Lace was very skilfully appliqued onto the finest silk and she knew they must have been made in China.

She did not say anything.

Lo Nu went to the cupboard in the cabin and brought out the most beautiful gown Velda had ever seen.

It was of white chiffon with frill upon frill of shadow lace round the hem.

Lace also decorated the puffed sleeves and the décolletage.

Velda gave a little gasp, then she said rather weakly:

'That is . . . not . . . my gown!'

'You no clothes left of your own,' Lo Nu said quietly.

'Why not?' Velda asked.

'Dr. Wang give orders evlything you own be burned.'

Velda knew it was because of the infection.

At the same time, she thought that once again Mike Medway had got his own way.

She had to accept what clothes he would give her, otherwise go naked.

'He is so devious!' she told herself.

Yet she could not help being thrilled by the gown.

It fitted her perfectly and was so beautiful it could only have been made by Chinese fingers.

When Nurse had fastened the buttons at her back Velda looked at herself in the mirror.

She knew she looked very different from how she had ever looked before.

She wondered if Mike Medway would notice and what he would think.

She hoped he would not notice she was still very thin.

At the same time she was happy and excited.

Her eyes seemed to fill her face and shine like the stars which she could see coming out in the sky.

There was a knock on her door, and the younger Nurse opened it.

Cheng handed her something and she brought it to Velda.

It was a wreath very much in the shape of the one she had worn at the fireworks party.

Now it was made of small orchids and tiny white frangipani flowers.

It was so lovely that she gave a little cry of delight when she put it on.

She had wondered if Mike Medway had admired her in the Chinese wreath she had worn with her Chinese costume.

Now she thought he must have done.

That was why he had sent her a wreath to wear tonight, so that she would look pretty as they dined.

One of the Nurses had gone from her cabin, and now she came back to say:

'They leady now, wait for Governor come aboard.'

'The Governor?'

Velda felt her heart sink.

So she was not to be alone with Mike Medway at dinner.

He was entertaining the Governor, Sir John Pope-Hennessy and perhaps other people as well.

She felt all her elation sweep away.

Then before she could say anything the door opened and Jimmy came in.

He was dressed in a smart suit that she had not seen before and he said as if it had been rehearsed:

'Uncle Mike says I'm to take you to the Saloon where he is waiting for you.'

He put out his hand and Velda gave him hers.

'That will be fun,' she said, 'and you look very smart!'

'It is my new suit,' Jimmy said proudly.

As if he remembered Mike Medway was waiting, he said:

'Come along, Velda! I will show you where to go.'

'Thank you,' Velda said to the Nurses.

They went out of the cabin.

Jimmy was holding her hand very tightly and pulling her forward.

Outside the Saloon Cheng was waiting.

He was holding in his hand a small bouquet of the same flowers as Velda wore on her head.

'Flowers flom Master, Missie Armstlong,' he said as he presented them.

'How very kind!' Velda replied. 'Thank you Cheng.'

He opened the door of the Saloon and Jimmy drew her forward.

Then as she stepped inside Velda gave a little gasp.

She could hardly believe what she saw.

She thought she was very stupid not to have guessed what Mike Medway was planning.

But how could she have thought of anything so incredible, so utterly and completely unbelievable?

The Bishop from the Church of St. John was standing at the end of the Saloon.

Behind him had been erected a small altar on which there were six lighted candles and a gold cross.

In front of him were two satin cushions.

Seated facing the altar was the Governor.

There was no one else in the Saloon except Mike Medway standing waiting for her.

Proudly Jimmy drew her forward until she stood beside him.

When his eyes met hers she felt as if fireworks were flaring up into the sky and she was going with them.

Except for the throbbing of the engines, it was very quiet in the Master Cabin as Velda and Mike Medway walked into it.

It would have been difficult after the ceremony to behave normally.

The Governor and the Bishop had stayed with them for the Wedding Breakfast which was of course a Chinese dinner.

Bishop Thimoleon Raimondi was a bearded giant of a man who had originally come to Hong Kong from the Milan Mission.

He had become the First Vicar Apostolic of Hong Kong and been a tremendous help to the Governor in his attempts to give the Chinese community equality.

But it was Jimmy who seemed to do most of the talking.

He chatted away excitedly about his horse, about *The Sea Dragon* and the games he had learnt from the Chinese seamen.

Everybody seemed to be laughing and Velda knew they were happy, as she was, but none of it seemed real.

She could not believe it was happening and that Mike Medway's wedding-ring was on the third finger of her left hand.

She was his wife!

Why had he not told her?

Why had he not prepared her for something she had never expected?

Above all, she had never thought it possible.

He had wanted to surprise her but why had he wanted to marry her?

Above all how was he able to do so?

It was the one question that was uppermost in her mind.

Then all she could think of was how handsome he was and every nerve in her body vibrated towards him.

She was almost sure he felt the same.

As if they knew they were not wanted, the Governor and the Bishop left immediately after the wedding-breakfast.

Jimmy went with them.

'My sister and her husband arrived today,' Sir John Pope Hennessy announced during dinner.

'How nice for you,' Velda said.

'He is to be one of my *Aides-de-Camp*,' the Governor went on, 'and their son who is seven years old will go to the same School as Jimmy.'

He smiled as he went on:

'I think the two boys will enjoy being together while you are on your honeymoon, and there are plenty of things to keep them amused at Government House.'

Velda glanced at Mike.

She knew by the expression in his eyes that he had arranged this so that they could be alone.

'How very kind of you,' she said demurely to Sir John.

Jimmy was so excited at the idea of travelling with the Governor with a Cavalry escort that he almost forgot to kiss her goodbye.

When they had gone Velda and Mike were alone in the Saloon.

She looked at him and everything she wished to say was swept out of her mind.

All she wanted was that she should be in his arms, and that he should kiss her.

Instead he took her by the hand back to the Master Cabin where she had been for so long.

As she entered it she saw that while they had been away it had been decorated with flowers.

There were garlands over the portholes and the head-board of the bed was covered with white orchids.

There were huge jars of white lilies and Chinese vases were filled with white roses.

Velda could hardly take it all in.

She was waiting, as if for the rising of the curtain, for Mike to tell her what had happened.

He shut the door, pulled off the smart, tight-fitting evening-coat he had been wearing and threw it on a chair.

Then, as she had wanted, he put his arms around her and drew her close against him.

'Now at last,' he said, 'you are mine, and we need have no more arguments about it.'

She laughed because it was not what she had expected him to say.

'H.how . . . has this happened . . . how could it . . . happen?'

'That is something I am going to tell you all about,' he said, 'but not now. All you need to know is that I was free to marry you. I have been a widower for over four years!'

She looked at him in astonishment.

'But . . . no one knew . . . you never said . . .'

'Because I had vowed never to marry again,' he interrupted, 'it suited me to be as everybody thought, still tied to the woman who was my wife.'

Velda gave a little exclamation.

'But I . . . thought! . . .' she began.

'I know,' he said gently, 'and you will have to forgive me. All that matters now . . . my darling is that you are mine, and I will never lose you!'

Then he kissed her, passionately, demandingly, possessively.

She felt the lightning streak through her.

As he drew her closer and still closer she felt that nobody could know such rapture and not die of the wonder of it.

She could feel her whole body saying what she had said so often:

'I love you . . . I love you!'

He was kissing her until she was a part of him and they were indivisible.

It was a glory which carried them both up into the sky.

A long time later when the engines were quiet Velda knew that once again they had reached the island where they had anchored before.

'Is this . . . really true . . . or have I died?' she asked, 'and . . . found you . . . in Heaven?'

'It is Heaven,' Mike said in his deep voice, 'but we are both alive, my precious darling, and like a Fairy Story, we shall live happily ever after.'

'You are . . . quite sure . . . of that?'

She moved a little closer to him and hid her face against his neck as she whispered:

'Suppose . . . you grow . . . bored with me . . . and perhaps now . . . because I am so . . . ignorant . . . I have . . . disappointed you?'

He moved her a little way from him so that he could look at her in the moonlight that was coming through the portholes.

It had turned the cabin into a Fairyland that seemed was part of their dream.

'Do you really believe I could ever feel like that about you?' he asked. 'You are perfect because you are a part of me.'

'Are you . . . sure . . . of that?' Velda asked.

'I tried to run away from you,' he admitted, 'I tried to forget you, but to lose you would have been like losing my arm or leg, and of course, my heart!'

He gave a little laugh before he added:

'I never knew I had one before, but I assure you it has hurt me abominably before it drew me back to Hong Kong and then I thought you might have died!'

'And you . . . minded? You . . . really minded?'

He pulled her roughly to his chest.

'I nearly went mad!' he said. 'If you had died I would have been crippled – deformed – no longer myself.'

He kissed the softness of her skin before he said:

'You told me that you believed in immortality, and that, my precious love, is what we shall achieve together. You are not only mine now, but for all eternity.'

'That is . . . what I . . . want to be,' Velda said, 'but because . . . you are so . . . wonderful . . . so grand . . . I am afraid I might . . . fail you.'

'All you have to do,' Mike replied, 'is to love me.'

'I do love you! I love you with all of me!' Velda cried. 'With all my heart . . . my soul and my . . . body!'

She whispered the last word a little shyly.

He thought as he drew her closer still that he had never known such happiness.

It had been an experience he had never had before to touch somebody as completely innocent and pure as Velda.

He had been very gentle in case he should frighten her.

But he knew the ecstasy they found together was but the beginning of the spiritual as well as the physical rapture they would discover in the future.

'You are mine!' he said fiercely as she quivered against him. 'Mine, and there are a million things for us to do because we are together, but which I could not do without you.'

'Do you . . . mean that? Do you . . . really mean . . . it?' Velda asked. 'I feel because I am so . . . insignificant and unimportant that I can give you

'. . . very little . . . while you can give me . . . so much!'

'I can give you material things,' Mike said, 'but you will give me something I have never had, and which I have missed instinctively, without being aware of it.'

'What is that?' Velda asked.

'Three things,' he replied, 'three things I told myself I did not want, but which now I know I cannot live without.'

She waited, feeling that their happiness was throbbing round them like the fragrance of the flowers.

'First I want a home,' Mike said softly, 'secondly I want a son, and thirdly, and most important of all I want a wife who is all mine and who will think only of me!'

Velda gave a little cry.

'Oh, darling, I want to give you all those things! I know that if we pray hard enough, you will have them all, and they will be as perfect as you want them to be.'

'I already have you,' Mike said in his deep voice, 'and you, my precious, are completely and absolutely perfect!'

'Even if I am too thin?' Velda asked.

He gave a little laugh.

'My Chef has orders to fatten you up, and I am sure he is praying to *Tso Kwan* that he will not fail!'

Velda laughed too. Then she said:

'Oh, darling, darling Mike . . . I love you . . . I love you! How could I ever have imagined that I would marry anybody so wonderful or so kind and . . . understanding?'

It flashed through Mike's mind that no man could be more fortunate.

146

No man could have more luck than to marry Velda who had never wanted anything from him but his heart.

He knew that the women he had thought of as he had been trying to forget her had faded into the mists of time.

He knew that everything he had done to amuse himself when he was not working had brought him no real happiness.

He had not known the ecstasy he had felt just looking at Velda when she was in a coma.

And when he kissed her hand as she was getting better.

He had not been aware that he could feel as he felt now.

He was so happy that he was no longer on earth but high in the sky amongst the stars.

He had found love.

Love was greater than any other of his possessions, his fortune, his ships, his treasures.

If he ever had to choose between them and Velda, he would not hesitate.

She was everything he had always wanted but he had been unable to express it even to himself.

She was like the flowers that surrounded them.

At the same time she was still a bud, and it was his love that would make her open her petals.

Then she would become a blossom as he brought her to womanhood.

'You are mine, mine!' he said aloud. 'I will kill anyone who tried to take you from me!'

Now Velda put her hand up to draw his head down to hers.

'I am completely and absolutely yours . . . and I can only thank God for . . . letting me find you.'

The little throb in her voice was very moving.

Then as Mike kissed her wildly, fiercely, demandingly, she felt the lightning seep through her.

They were no longer human.

They themselves were gods; moving together into an Eternity where there was only love and nothing else was of any importance.